POETIC
JUSTICE

BOOKS IN THIS SERIES

Poetic Justice: The Dawning
Poetic Justice: Oxford

POETIC JUSTICE

OXFORD

FRAN RAYA

The Book Guild Ltd

First published in Great Britain in 2019 by
The Book Guild Ltd
9 Priory Business Park
Wistow Road, Kibworth
Leicestershire, LE8 0RX
Freephone: 0800 999 2982
www.bookguild.co.uk
Email: info@bookguild.co.uk
Twitter: @bookguild

Copyright © 2019 Fran Raya

The right of Fran Raya to be identified as the author of this
work has been asserted by her in accordance with the
Copyright, Design and Patents Act 1988.

All rights reserved. No part of this publication may be
reproduced, transmitted, or stored in a retrieval system, in any form or by any means,
without permission in writing from the publisher, nor be otherwise circulated in
any form of binding or cover other than that in which it is published and without
a similar condition being imposed on the subsequent purchaser.

This work is entirely fictitious and bears no resemblance to any persons living or dead.

Typeset in Aldine401 BT

Printed and bound in Great Britain by CPI Group (UK) Ltd, Croydon, CR0 4YY

ISBN 978 1912881 765

British Library Cataloguing in Publication Data.
A catalogue record for this book is available from the British Library.

*I wish to dedicate this book to my vivid imagination
and to The Book Guild for letting it run riot.*

*Also, to the readers who read the first book in the series
and who have requested the second.*

Here it is.

*Read it with the lights on.
Randal Forbes is unstoppable.*

*Best wishes to you all,
Fran Raya*

Randal Forbes calls his dynamic, telepathic powers 'the gift' and uses them to destroy those who suspect his paranormal leanings. He has compelling slate-grey eyes with yellow glints, which radiate when aroused. He has left behind a trail of homicidal atrocity and is now under suspicion but his involvement is very hard to prove, because he is rarely at the elimination scene, just in his victims' heads.

In this second book of the series, Randal has been accepted as a student at Beaumont College, Oxford. He is a genius, extraordinarily attractive, and is well on the way to becoming a celebrated author.

Although fractionally bisexual, there is one girl who completely captures his soul.

There are new 'enemies' to deal with but in Randal's mind, each psychic murder is fully justified.

Randal Forbes has a dark side so powerful that only someone with a similar gift will be able to challenge him. But who would dare?

1

Randal Forbes opened the window in his room and looked down on the city of Oxford below. He breathed in its historical splendour and could well understand why it had been home to generations of writers, artists, poets and philosophers. He had been at Beaumont College for one month and in that short time felt as if he was part of the city walls. He had never seen so many towers, pinnacles and domes within an area of less than half a square mile and told his close friend and protector, Clive Hargreaves, the night before.

"Do you also know that Oxford and Cambridge share the distinction of being the seat of only a small number of universities in Europe which have preserved the medieval collegiate system? How cool is that?" he enthused.

Randal viewed it all as a great architectural treasure containing examples of every building style in England from the eleventh century onwards.

"Mind you, I don't dig that strong religious vibe that goes back to the Dominican friars and those frisky Franciscans. Thankfully both of those whopping great churches have almost disappeared," he added, with a luminous glint in his mesmerising eyes.

"Not entirely, others have sprung up," corrected Clive bravely, at the risk of inciting Randal's displeasure.

"Doesn't matter. The ghosts of their religious benefactors have already tuned in to 'the gift' and their disapproval just amuses me," he smiled. That smile.

Clive swallowed hard as Randal's charismatic presence swamped him. He looked so seductive and ready for any challenge.

"You know, Clive, this is the perfect place for me. I belong here; for now, at least. There's so much scope for my work. I've got loads of ideas for my writing outside of the academic bubble. I can't stop scribbling away. I'm itching to make my mark and that's exactly what I'm going to do."

Randal had everything under control. In the spring of 1976, he had received an unconditional offer from Beaumont College. His report from Redwood private school was glowing and he had secured a place for himself without waiting for A-level results. Clive had received a conditional offer which meant that it was his for the taking, provided he achieved the grades required.

Randal had kept his secret psychic promise by subtly entering Clive's head and mentally giving him the helping hand that he needed to reach his goal. As a result, Clive found himself alongside Randal, at Beaumont, studying English literature.

They were given their own rooms in the college itself, but a short distance apart. In their freshers' week, they found their feet rather quickly through the camaraderie of the other students, simply by being new undergraduates together.

There were three terms during each year, each of eight weeks, namely Michaelmas, Hilary and Trinity and on Friday, 1st October 1976, they began their first term together in their new academic home. Randal was relishing every moment of his fantastic adventure and Clive was savouring every second of his time with Randal.

Randal had contacted Alison Whitaker in London, as soon as he had settled in. She had leased a flat close to the Royal Academy which was now her home base. She had kept in touch with him all the while they had been apart. She knew he would sail through his examinations but the only reservation she had, was the fact that Clive would still be with him, in close proximity, possibly for the next three years.

Alison did not have anything against Clive personally. In fact, he made her laugh, and was always polite. Clive bothered her simply because she knew that he was in love with Randal and she was not quite sure where it was all heading. She thought of him as Randal's shadow and had been on the verge of actually asking him if there was anything going on that she should know about. Then she remembered the hot looks between her and Randal at their last meeting and knew he had never looked at Clive with that same intensity. She mentally shook her head.

No way! Randal wants me badly even though nothing's happened yet. Clive's passion for Randal is so one-sided and I feel sorry for him. Randal's not bisexual.

Clive was deeply jealous when he found out that Randal and Alison had been in touch with each other and he tried to control his feelings.

Don't be ungrateful. I really can't believe that I achieved such high grades. Is it such a big deal if he hooks up with Alison occasionally? I don't have to be there, so stop all the tortured thoughts. It could have been a lot worse. I might have been parted from him for the next year. Well I'm not. So, lighten up!

Being in love with Randal was a heavy cross to bear and Clive knew there would be others in his idol's life and bed. It was imperative to work out a regime against becoming too possessive. He knew that Randal would run a hundred miles away if he tried to tie him down. He was a free-spirited phenomenon and needed more space than a lesser mortal. He must not be hampered with weakness and being in the inner sanctum of Randal's kingdom was as close as he could possibly be.

In the month they had been at Beaumont, Randal was making his indelible mark on the college clubs and societies. The other fellows were hugely impressed.

"Just watch out for the red-haired, new-boy genius, reading English lit," alerted one student to another.

"Who's that then?"

"Forbes. Randal Forbes. It's a name to remember."

Randal was very sports-minded and had joined the boat club, training as a freshman, but unfortunately the weather had put the river in flood for the first few weeks of the Michaelmas term. Nevertheless, his name had been noted as the best rower in his novice eight.

"I'm so proud of you," fawned Clive, "more than ever."

"You know me; centre of attention and not ashamed to admit it."

For added effect he had joined The Beaumont Players with the intention of becoming internally famous in the college dramatics, both as an actor and writer of new scripts.

★★★

On one of his days in between tutorials, Randal decided to explore the city on his own. There was a slight nip in the air so he wrapped his scarf around his neck to keep out the cold. The students rode bicycles and Randal was no exception but today he wanted to investigate on foot.

He had passed his driving test easily before he moved to Oxford, so his parents had bought him a car as a gift for his eighteenth birthday, and to acknowledge his scholarship. He had no immediate use for it as he could ride his bike to most places.

He gazed upward and saw that the skyline was crowded with Gothic towers and steeples. As he travelled further, he noted that each college was built around two or three quadrangles, with a chapel hall, library and walled gardens. He studied them all closely and nodded his head in silent affirmation of their presence.

Randal stood still and listened. A jumble of desperate sounds snaked their way into the ever-open portals of his receptive mind. A series of vivid pictures flashed in and out of his head and he winced, as the sight, sound and smell of violent bloodshed filtered through his brain, bringing with it the full horrors of the past.

This is the famous 'town and gown' friction; a bloodbath with students fighting and the townspeople arrogant and resentful; the Massacre of St. Scholastica Day in 1354. I can see it all and feel their hostility. Will these visions ever leave me alone? I guess not. It's all part and parcel of 'the gift'. I have to take the good with the bad and file it all away.

Randal knew that the battle resulted in sixty-two students being killed and the rest of them were driven away from the town.

I could have stopped this had I lived then and I would have changed the course of history. I have the power to do so. I would have worked with Edward II who was sickened by the fatal disruption to academic life.

Randal turned his head from side to side, tuning in to the King's displeasure, and heard him issue the university with a new charter which effectively gave it control over Oxford for the next five hundred years.

His mind was its own historical manual. Not only could he hear the voices of the town's past peerage but he could also see their impressive images, dressed in their relevant splendour and flamboyance, with their regal sense of occasion. He revelled in the ambience and felt its majesty pumping through his veins.

This had rapidly become his new spiritual home, which pampered his aestheticism. Its influence painted poetic pictures in his current book of verse. His mind soaked up his academic studies like a scholarly sponge. His opinions became widely sought after and his sensuality burned its way into all who rallied round him. As always, there were those who were drawn in and others who felt uncomfortable by his penetrating gaze. He frowned.

I have to be in total control of my destiny. 'The gift' will guide me along the way and I must listen to its advice. I've always been able to run before I could walk but I must trust in my benefaction. The voice in my boyhood dream told me there will be enemies and I will know them when they come. I have to be aware and remain tireless in my pursuit of excellence in homage to my standing. I just have to be.

Alison hummed her latest musical creation as she drove her car along the roads leading into Oxford town centre. She had arranged to meet Randal at Beaumont but he had kept her identity secret, telling her to go to the Lodge around lunchtime. Although he had been in touch with her by letter and telephone, Randal had not actually seen her in the flesh since her surprise appearance at his Aunty Dottie's wedding in April 1975.

She remembered the way he had reacted when she had walked in unexpectedly. All of a sudden, the boy had become a man, and the feeling of sexual longing she had experienced from his sensual gaze was swamping.

She had always known there was a pull between them, right from the moment she had set eyes on him in her parents' confectionary shop, when he was ten years old. From that day onwards, she had felt instinctively that she would have to wait for him to grow up. He had enclosed a recent photograph of himself in his latest letter and she had held her breath at the sight of his blatant sensuality.

She thought he was the most stunning example of masculinity she had ever seen and she had met many attractive young men in her own musical circle. Randal exuded sex appeal in spades and the thought of meeting him again, face to face, made her dizzy with desire.

I've got so much to tell you about the years in between. I know you'll freak out when you hear that I'm appearing with the London Philharmonic Orchestra at the Albert Hall and performing an original piano piece, in the presence of royalty.

She wanted to see his expression when she told him because he would bathe in her acclaim, as if it was his own. Randal had instilled a confidence in her, a long time before her initial success story. They were both climbing the same progressive ladder to the very top of their particular trees.

Alison had been to Oxford previously on business but had never found the time to browse around its historical features. Now she had the opportunity.

I can't wait to see him. His letters are so amazing and he makes everything sound important, especially his life in the college itself. He said he would introduce me as a family member. He's so thoughtful, keeping my true vocation under wraps, and maybe, just maybe, he has his own reasons for keeping me to himself?

Her heart skipped several beats at the idea of intimacy between them and she squirmed with desire. She was not on her own with those thoughts.

Randal had waited eight years for this moment and now he was more than ready to seal his love for the only girl who had ever stirred his soul. It did not matter that he was approaching his nineteenth birthday and that the world was his oyster, because other women just fed his greedy ego.

Alison was his kindred spirit and it was written a long time ago. She had been there in every transition. This time she was five years older in material years but really, they were both very ancient, meeting up repeatedly in time and space. And now it was time for the first time.

All over again.

He was waiting at the Lodge for her, his tall frame leaning against the archaic walls of its entrance. Their eyes found each other and time stood still, as if everything else around them had been erased, like a blackboard rubber blanking out a redundant chalked message. For a moment she felt unable to move as her body responded to his physical perfection. Slowly her senses came back to life and she felt her limbs jerk forward unsteadily into his embrace.

They hugged each other tightly and she had to stand on her toes to wrap her arms around his neck. He kissed her hot cheek and she felt his shapely lips against her face, leaving her with a strong desire for a more intimate gesture of affection. He moved slightly away and looked down at her burnished hair, which framed her lovely face, and held his breath at the depth of emotion in her amber eyes. She looked incredible.

"You're so beautiful," he whispered as he stroked a piece of loose hair away that had fallen into her eyes.

"Am I?" she just about replied, but her tongue seemed to stiffen in her mouth and she was unable to say anything more.

"You are. Now, where have you parked? We need to get your luggage," he suggested, getting back to practicalities, a bit too soon for her liking.

He put his arm around her shoulder as they walked over to her car and opened the boot.

"It's the brown leather suitcase. I've everything I need for the weekend," she instructed.

"Have you now?" he murmured and her heart stalled.

Randal carried it to the college gates and Alison could not appreciate the historical beauty around her as she followed him along the ancient winding passages. He was inspired by her presence and talked excitedly about Beaumont but all she could see was the shapely masculine shoulders in front of her and his long, muscular legs as he strode along the corridors in complete control of his environment.

"Here we are then," he said and opened the door to his room for the next forty-eight hours.

Alison knew that in a building as old as Beaumont that she would not be living in the lap of modern luxury, but she was totally unprepared for the starkness and gloom that was in front of her. She looked around and saw an old battered leather settee, no doubt abused by the many students and guests over the years. Two wooden chairs were tucked inside the hollows of a scratched oak table, which had seen far better days.

Books and papers were scattered everywhere and a discarded academic robe lay crushed in the corner. Through the door on her left was a bathroom and toilet. There was what appeared to be a recess in the wall but when she looked more closely, she realised that inside the cramped area there was a bed. The partition housed the original old brick, with no decoration to disguise its monastic appearance and she thought it would be like sleeping in a tomb.

Randal's lips twitched with amusement when he saw her adverse reaction to it all. He had told her exactly what to expect in his letters but she had still insisted on staying with him at Beaumont, rather than booking into a hotel which would have catered to her creature comforts.

Her disapproval was entertaining him as she tried to make herself believe that her surroundings looked better than they actually were. By the expression on her face, she had failed to convince herself. The sound of Randal's laughter jolted her out of her dilemma.

"Well I did try to warn you," he teased.

"I know you did, but not nearly enough!" she objected.

"I can always book you into The Randolph. It costs an arm and a leg though."

"The Randolph? Sounds like your name," she jested.

"Come here, gorgeous snob," he said, holding out his arms, "let's put a smile back on your stunning face."

Suddenly the mood changed dramatically and Alison forgot to breathe when she saw his startling grey eyes glitter with restrained sexual tension. His gaze bore into hers and she felt the heat between her legs as his expression intensified.

In some kind of slow motion, she watched him remove her jacket. His face advanced towards hers and then his lips came down on her own. The kiss was electric and her heart started to thump against her ribs as he pulled her closer to his hard frame. His mouth moved round towards her slender neck and she felt him nuzzle the sensitive area, leaving her breathless with longing.

"I want you," he breathed thickly in her ear and she swayed to the side as her legs threatened to give way. "I need you," he added raggedly against her eardrum and she thought she was going to pass out, as he held her tightly, in the strong circle of his arms.

"Lie down; lie down here with me," he almost begged.

Alison was on fire. She put up no resistance when he pulled them both down on the battered old couch. He stretched himself out against her, so that they lay side by side, and kissed her passionately. She felt his hard erection against the top of her thighs and she pushed up against him so that she could feel its full impact.

She had never in all her young life acted so wantonly but Randal had this devastating effect on her senses. *This* is what she had always wanted and *that* was why she had found so many other men lacking.

His technique was much too good for him to be a stranger to the art of lovemaking. At the back of her mind she felt upset at the idea of him with another girl. She had wanted to be his first but his touch was far too experienced for that to be so.

She felt his hand moving under her blouse and it blotted out any more thoughts as his long, slim fingers found their way to her breast.

She stopped him momentarily and took off her top in a feverish manner in order to leave the way absolutely clear for his touch. He unhooked the back of her bra and slipped the straps off her smooth shoulders, sliding them down her arms, and removing the rest out of the way. His breathing became laboured as he fondled her firm, full breasts, feasting on the sight of their exquisite form. Alison groaned as he bent his head, teasing her with the gentle circling of his tongue around the stiff peak and then taking the full nipple in his mouth, sucking hard on its tip. She moaned even louder when he did the same thing to her other breast but it was not enough.

"Love me, Randal," she whispered urgently as she felt him unzipping her skirt and dragging it down over her hips.

"I will and I do," he replied in a strange, thick voice which only excited her all the more as he unfastened his jeans.

They undressed each other with an urgency born out of years of waiting and at long last their two naked forms lay side by side. His feverish eyes and hands kept running along the whole of her length, not knowing where to rest or touch, in his desperation to make her his own. It was no good. He had to be inside her and anything else would have to wait. There would be time for experimental pleasure later on. He did not want to violate her but his need was so great that it was difficult to remain in control.

She moved on to her back and he mounted her, his body heat telling her that he was more than ready. His knee pushed open her already parted legs and he positioned himself for immediate entry. She felt the tip of his manhood throbbing against her wetness and squealed as she perceived the first thrust of full penetration. They had both imagined this a thousand times, how it would be between them, but nothing had prepared them for such an overpowering experience.

Feelings of love, lust, tenderness and passion fused together in a powerhouse of emotion and they were lost to the world around them.

She felt his urgent movements inside her body. She could tell by the way he was pushing more forcefully into her that he was reaching boiling point. He grew even harder as his rhythm speeded up and she matched every lunge. He knew that he could not sustain it any longer and felt the beginnings of his orgasm building up towards its intense release. She felt him climax inside her and at the same time she reached her own rapture, panting shamelessly with the release.

Some five minutes later they were still breathing heavily in the aftermath of their lovemaking. Randal was overcome by the depth of feeling that she had evoked in his breast. He knew that if he lived to be a very old man, he would never find her equal. She completely eradicated any cruel, detached or dispassionate emotions inside him, bringing out a tenderness that was at total odds with his malevolent reprisals.

He felt her stir beneath him and she caressed his shoulders, pressing up against him wantonly.

"Again, Randal," she pleaded.

Incredulously he felt himself harden and the whole passionate ritual began all over again. And yet again.

Some hours later they decided to face the outside world. As far as Alison was concerned, they could have spent the whole weekend on that shapeless, old couch and she would not have offered one word of protest.

"I'd love to stay here, like this. Forever," she whispered.

"Would you now? We've got two whole days together and years of loving to look forward to," he murmured against her lips.

Alison shivered slightly as he got up from the settee and took his body heat with him. The room was somewhat chilly as he gathered his discarded clothes together. She studied his naked form and saw how well endowed he was as he pulled up his briefs. She felt a quiver of excitement run down her spine as she remembered how good he felt inside her.

She admired his long, muscular legs as he stepped into his jeans and fastened them over his firm, flat stomach. A dark blue velvet shirt completed the outfit and her heart flipped at the sight of his smooth, hard chest behind the buttons. He brushed his thick, coppery red hair in the mirror and it flopped over his forehead in an unruly fringe, which succeeded in making him look boyish and rakish at the same time.

"Seen enough?" he teased.

He glided over to the couch and sat on the edge, surveying her nudity through worshipping eyes.

"I love you and want to marry you," he said unexpectedly, as he stroked the inside of her thigh.

She swallowed hard, completely taken aback. He helped her up and held her nakedness against his fully clothed body, clasping her shapely bottom with both hands and pulling her towards him seductively.

"Get dressed, you'll catch cold," he said gently and kissed the tip of her nose.

She gazed into his unusual grey eyes and saw nothing but tenderness. She would not have believed the torture that those same alien eyes had inflicted upon his victims; those multiple homicidal crimes of the worst kind.

She knew they both had much to achieve before they took their inevitable vows and she did not need any ceremony to seal her love for him.

"You've not even unpacked your case yet," he smiled.

"I was too busy," she pouted suggestively.

She found an outfit she had packed and put it on. She zipped up her green suede jacket over the same-coloured jumpsuit and slung her leather bag over her right shoulder. Suddenly she was ravenous and realised she had not eaten since early morning.

Randal knew beyond any shadow of a doubt that throughout the coming night she would feel a different kind of hunger and he would more than satisfy that need.

★★★

Clive sat on his bed flicking through some notes from his last tutorial. His concentration kept waning and he could not absorb any of the information. This was going to be one hell of a weekend to get through and he felt his eyes prick with unshed tears. He had been told to keep his distance while Alison was visiting and although Randal was polite in his explanation, it all boiled down to the fact that he wanted Clive out of the way.

The radio was playing an old Beatles track and Clive wallowed in his misery as he listened to the familiar lyrics of *'You Really Got a Hold on Me'*. The words reflected his feelings for Randal to such a degree, that his sorrow was even more magnified by their meaning. It was far too much to endure, as the tears threatened to flow.

He could not stand it any more and flung his notes across the room, jumping up quickly from the bed to switch off the song. His emotions were dictating his actions and against his better judgement, he decided to go to the students' union bar, where he would meet up with some of his new-found friends and hopefully get so drunk, he would forget what he did not want to remember. He grabbed his coat and left the room, taking his anger out on the door by slamming it so hard that it nearly parted with its hinges.

The nights were drawing in and although it was only six thirty, the town was well illuminated. His hands felt cold as he put them in the deep pockets of his windjammer and headed in the right direction.

"Hi there, Clive! How you doing, man?" asked one of the revellers as he walked into the main room, which was warm and welcoming.

"I'm pissed off, that's how I am," Clive shot back with a scowl and the student just shrugged as he flounced away.

The air was thick with the smell of beer and cigarette smoke. He had to fight his way to the bar but it did not matter. The more noise and chaos around him the better.

"Why don't you join us in the corner? There's a spare seat at our table," said a familiar face from his course. "Go and sit there, the drinks are on me."

Clive nodded his head in agreement, glad of the invitation. Anything to get the mental image of Randal and Alison fornicating out of his ransacked head.

Marcus Pennington made his way through the ever-increasing mass of bodies with two glasses of whisky and a small bottle of Coke. He had wanted to get Clive on his own for a while now but he always seemed to be glued to Randal Forbes, like his conjoined twin.

Marcus thought that Randal was outstanding but it was Clive who had touched his heart. He instinctively knew that Clive and Randal were together and that Clive was obsessed with his auburn-haired Adonis, in more ways than one.

However, tonight he was going solo, and by the solemn expression on his face, was decidedly up for grabs.

Clive patted the empty seat next to him as Marcus reached the crowded table. He acknowledged the gesture. Clive felt hot and bothered as he removed his jacket and hung it over the back of his chair. He ignored the other students purposefully.

"Cheers," said Marcus as he poured some Coke into Clive's whisky.

"I feel like shit," mumbled Clive, stating the obvious to his attentive listener, polishing off his drink like it was lemonade. He looked very depressed as he stared into the bottom of his empty glass, offering no explanation for his sour mood.

"Would you like to talk about it?" asked Marcus, trying to break the ice and get Clive to open up.

"I just want another drink and then after that another," grimaced Clive, lighting up a cigarette.

"I see," acknowledged Marcus, as he reached under the table for a plastic bag which contained some items he had purchased that same afternoon. He bent down and searched underneath the large sliced loaf of bread, crumbly Cheshire cheese and Bakewell tart.

"Here we are," he specified as he pulled out a large bottle of brandy. "For medicinal purposes. I must have known you were coming. To your health, Clive," he added, pouring the same into both glasses and raising his in a friendly gesture.

Marcus was good company. His quick brain and dry wit acted like an antidepressant on Clive's unhappiness, ridding him of his saturnine expression and replacing the hollowness in his chest with a sense of hope.

Clive looked up and began to really notice his saviour, seeing him properly for the first time. He was of average height with long dark hair and deep blue eyes. His face was wide with well-defined cheekbones and a slightly aquiline nose rested above his bow-shaped mouth. His smile revealed a gap in between his two front teeth, which gave him an appealing impish grin.

His voice was very cultured and it was obvious from his whole deportment that he was from a wealthy background but there was absolutely no trace of snobbery in his attitude to those around him. Clive began to join in with the crowd.

"Have another one, Marcus can afford it. His parents are Lord and Lady Pennington," intimated a fellow student and Clive was even more impressed.

His glass was repeatedly filled and he was beginning to feel very intoxicated. He knew he was well on the way to becoming paralytic but he carried on regardless. Life was not so bad after all and when Marcus put an arm around his shoulder, Clive liked the sensation.

Take that, Randal! You're not the only one allowed to have fun elsewhere you know.

Somebody told a joke and Clive staggered to his feet to slap the comedian on the back. He collided awkwardly with a girl and knocked her flying. He laughed at his clumsiness but his amusement did not last long when he saw that it was Alison on the floor. Worse still was the thunderous expression on Randal's face.

Through his drunken haze, Clive felt Randal push him out of the way to get to Alison who had fallen clumsily, banging her head on the back of a chair before she hit the ground. He rushed to her side to cradle her in his arms and was relieved to find that she was not so much injured as embarrassed by the whole situation. She rubbed the back of her skull.

"I'm OK, it's just a bump, so don't make a fuss."

Randal was blazing as he helped her up and brought a chair for her to sit on.

"I'm all right, really I am. It was an accident. He's had too much to drink so leave him alone to sober up," she said in a low voice when she saw Randal glare across at Clive with a peculiar luminous gaze in his eyes.

"I'm Marcus Pennington. Please let me buy you both a drink by way of an apology. After all I'm the guilty culprit here by plying Clive with too much booze."

"That won't be necessary," sniped Randal ungraciously but Alison accepted. Randal fell in with her wishes. Inwardly he was still vexed but she looked up at him with pleading eyes to accept the olive branch.

Clive felt ill. His stomach was churning with too much drink and pent-up emotion for one night. Marcus saw him lurch across the room with his hand in front of his mouth and followed him to make sure he was all right. He found him in the gents with his head over the toilet bowl being violently sick. Marcus pulled out several paper towels from the machine on the wall, walked over to the sink, and dampened them with cold water. He waited for Clive to stop retching and helped him out of the cubicle into the washroom. Clive looked ghastly and leaned heavily against his new friend for support. Marcus sat him in the corner and knelt in front of him, wiping his face and mouth with the cool compress.

"I want to die," groaned Clive, as the ceiling moved down onto the floor and the windows appeared to lift out of their frames in front of his blurred vision.

"Don't we all," replied Marcus with philosophical irony, borne out of too much self-analysis.

"I didn't mean to hurt her, she was just in the way," garbled Clive. "He'll hate me now. He wanted me out of his hair so he could screw her to death. That's why I got pissed. I can't stand it… I just can't stand it. I thought it would be OK but… but I just can't hack it!"

Clive burst into floods of drunken tears and Marcus vowed right there and then that he would do his very best to help him overcome his sorrow. He inwardly thought that Randal did not deserve his love; someone as sensitive and as kind as Clive needed that extra special attention.

Randal was obviously bisexual and could not be relied upon to give one hundred per cent dedication. Marcus knew he had a difficult task. Randal was out of the ordinary, both physically and mentally. He could understand how easily Clive had been caught in his web.

Someone had to save him and Marcus felt that he had been designated to do the job.

★★★

Clive did not see Randal until the Wednesday of the week after Alison had gone back to London. He had tried to corner him before that but every time he had called at his room he was out and all the messages he had left for him at the Lodge were totally ignored. Each rebuff brought with it more despondency and heartache.

Clive had skipped an important tutorial and he knew he would have to try harder to pull himself out of his deep depression. His mother and father had been in touch to say they were coming down to visit him in a fortnight, with Randal's parents. It was imperative that he sorted out 'the Alison problem' before that time.

He knew that Randal would be with the boat club, showing off to the other oarsmen, who were in training for the Christ Church Regatta. He reckoned that by now the activity would be nearly over, so he made his way there briskly through the fields before his nerve deserted him entirely. He saw quite a few boats on the water and strained his eyes into the distance to look for Randal's novice eight and found them on the far side to his right, rowing furiously towards the head of the river.

Clive sat on the bank and waited. When Randal was in hearing distance, he called out to him, waving his scarf to catch his attention.

"Hey there! I need to talk to you! It's important!"

Randal waved back in acknowledgement. Clive's heart lifted at his apparent willingness and it gave him the courage to name the venue.

"Meet me back at Beaumont in the Hall for lunch," he shouted through cupped hands.

"OK!" confirmed Randal with his thumb up in the air for extra approval.

The cox bawled out his orders once more and they turned around to retrace their route back to the boathouse. Clive watched until they became a speck in the distance and then disappeared out of sight. So far so good. Randal could not be that miffed or else he would have cold-shouldered him.

Maybe he's forgiven me for the accident. Perhaps I read too much into it and he's been very busy.

Clive looked at his watch and saw it was nearly midday. As if to recognise his raised spirits, the sun shone through the clouds and put a different complexion on the previous grey morning. He put his hands inside his coat pockets and whistled a favourite song, as he practically skipped along the path back to the college grounds.

He was far from sure how the meeting would go but he would do his best to restore the close and easy relationship between them both. He would apologise instantly for the unfortunate incident on that dreadful Saturday evening.

I need to know where I stand. Does he still want me now that Alison's back on the scene? I'm the only person who knows about 'the gift'. I'm his protector, not to mention his lover. Will he tell her about his telepathic powers? About his lust for psychic murder? About his bisexuality? I bloody well doubt it!

Randal had to take some responsibility for Clive's feelings. After all he had unlocked his deepest love and held the key to his heart.

It was noisy and crowded as they made their way to the long, ancient forms and tables in the Hall, carrying two plates of steaming hot food from the college canteen facilities. Randal was incredibly hungry from his sporting activity and tucked into his meal as if he had not eaten for a week. Clive just picked at the hotpot and pushed the layers of meat and potato around his plate, swallowing very little. He felt his appetite desert him just by being in Randal's immediate orbit. The clatter of plates and cutlery, plus the many conversations around them, put paid to any private discussion.

"I called round to your room last night but you were out," said Randal casually, causing Clive to nearly choke on the piece of meat he was forcing down his throat.

He swallowed it in one large chunk and reached for his glass of Coke to wash it down.

"Are you OK?" asked Randal, fully aware how his friend was feeling about the whole business in hand. He had finished his main course and was resting for a few minutes before he started on his pudding. He wiped his mouth with a paper napkin and waited for Clive to reply.

Clive took another large gulp of his drink and cleared his throat.

"Why didn't you get back to me when I left messages for you at the Lodge? Each time I returned to put another in your mail box, my previous ones hadn't even been collected. I wrote an apology to Alison, for the whole sorry incident last Saturday, and I wished her well. Why did you ignore me?" asked Clive in a hurt voice.

"I was angry with you for making a complete idiot of yourself. You were acting like a first-class piss artist and apart from sending Alison flying, I didn't think much of the company you were keeping," drawled Randal in a superior tone.

"Oh well, pardon me for living," replied Clive sarcastically. "Not only do you instruct me to give you and your precious girlfriend space, but you also want to choose the people who I should be keeping out of your way with! Well, it's not on! You've made the last few days hell and you know it!"

"Have I now?"

"You know you have! So, stop all the stupid mind games!" Clive glowered, throwing all caution to the wind, his bottom lip jutting outwards in a childish pout.

"Have you finished?" challenged Randal with a dangerous glint in his eyes.

A few of the other students had picked up on their disagreement. Until that moment, Clive had not realised just how loudly he was talking and that he could be heard above the general rowdiness of the crowd.

"Keep your voice down. They can hear you in the next college" scolded Randal as he pushed his unfinished apple crumble away. He wiped his mouth as he rose up from the bench to go.

"Let's get out of here. We need to talk," hissed Randal through clenched teeth.

"Yes let's!" demanded Clive, but Randal had already marched off.

Clive caught up with him outside.

"Slow down, I want to…"

"Shut it! I need to walk this off before we say anything!" warned Randal.

Clive bristled with indignation as they strode through the town, past all the other colleges until they reached Magdalen Bridge, where the river Cherwell flowed southwards to join the Thames. To the south-west of the bridge, between the river and the city wall, was Britain's first botanic garden, formerly known as the Physic Garden, which was part of the University Faculty of Medicine. Randal crossed the road and entered its gates, looking for a place to sit and air their differences. Clive was close behind him with much the same intention.

They found a secluded spot and sat down on a garden bench. Randal reached inside his coat pocket and brought out his cigarettes. He pulled two out of the pack, lighting them both, offering one to Clive. They inhaled deeply and blew out the smoke, silently watching it curling and weaving its way through the air. Clive opened his mouth to speak but Randal pipped him at the post.

"Now listen very carefully with no interruptions."

"Have I a choice? Do I ever have a choice?"

Randal turned to the side and held Clive's head in between his hands.

"When I first told you about 'the gift' and the burden and responsibility that came with it, I thought you understood my needs," he said in a serious voice, looking deep into Clive's hazel eyes.

Clive began to tremble. Not with fear but with longing. He let Randal continue.

"I'm not like you or anyone else I know. I've allowed you to get closer to me than any other person of our own sex. I can't give you more than that. I told you that I love Alison and that she's my female counterpart. I don't conform to human standards. I don't have the same morals or ethics. I'm a totally different animal, part human, part spirit, with a sexual appetite that's hungry for new experiences. This doesn't make me love Alison or you any less than I do. You must stop being possessive or trying to tie me down to a moment in time. I crave the freedom to nurture my expression and will reject anyone or anything that attempts to fence me in. Don't disappoint me, Clive, by showing me your weakness. I need your strength. I feed on your love and positive thoughts. I'll always be here for you but on my own terms. I would never stop you loving anyone else. You're free to choose," he concluded with an intense look on his stunning face, as if he was being driven by a higher expression.

"I promise to try and control my emotions. Just be patient with me, I'm still learning. I'll hide my jealousy but I can't stop it altogether. I love you and I always will. I'd die for you," pleaded Clive.

Randal smiled. He really did care for Clive and would reward his loyalty. He stroked his hair and whispered words of loving comfort in his ear and suggested they should spend the coming night together in his room. Clive felt the familiar heat rush though his body at the thought of rekindling his passion. They were closer than ever before.

2

Edward Forbes looked like the cat who had received a year's supply of double cream. He wore his paternal pride like a prestigious badge of office as he read his son's first published book of poems called *Poetic Justice*. It was Paul Hargreaves, Clive's father, who had instigated Randal's first big step up the literary ladder by showing his work to a variety of agents in the publishing field. Paul, who was a famous author, had admired Randal's creations for some time and was quite excited by the prospect of sponsoring his genius.

When both sets of parents had visited Randal and Clive in Oxford, a few days had been set aside in between tutorials to explore the city. It was then that Paul had first set eyes on the draft of Randal's complete collection to date. It was a highly descriptive poetical diary of his life, from childhood right through to the present day. Some poems were vividly realistic; others painted a surrealistic fantasia of words and pictures, that were almost hallucinatory in effect. Paul was enraptured by the imagery born out of Randal's own idiomatic style of verse. There was little difficulty in raising interest and a deal was clinched just before Christmas 1976, resulting in Randal travelling to London, to sign a contract, with Paul in tow.

So, it was in the Hilary Term at Beaumont College that Randal, at the age of nineteen, had developed into an outstanding student of English literature and became internally respected as an author in his own right.

"I'm so proud of you, and of my dad for paving the way. I know you'd have been successful regardless of his contacts but you chose to go down the accepted channels. You're so highly creative with an inborn gift for the written word, apart from the obvious!" raved Clive.

Randal's publishers had wasted no time in acquiring publicity for their latest signing.

"Have you seen these articles and reviews, Clive? Pretty damn good for a beginner huh?" said Randal with unashamed immodesty.

"What about Dr Gordon Swift, eh? Our eminent professor no less. He's only gone and invited your mum and dad to take tea with him in his room!"

"Yeah? How do you know that?" quizzed Randal.

"Because it's all around the college. You must be the only one who doesn't know. And here's me thinking you were psychic," quipped Clive.

Normally the only time that students became acquainted with a senior academic was in the first week, but they did not have much to do with them on a daily basis. Edward and Margaret were thrilled to be asked within the walls of such high academic accomplishment. They bathed in the ambience and the reflected glory of their son's triumph. Randal was pleased with the whole scenario. Things were heading in the right direction with perfect timing. He was being courted by the top people in key positions. He could hear the voice in his dream telling him that he would achieve fame and recognition as he had done in every lifetime.

Then he would fuse 'the gift' with his ambition and generate a creative wonderland in every corner of the world.

★★★

Back in Cheshire, Dr Patrick Shaw had purchased three copies of *Poetic Justice*. He gave one to his wife, Victoria, who was Randal's former nanny and eternal admirer, passed the other over to Chief Inspector Leonard Galloway for his attention and kept the third copy to study carefully in his spare time. He thought that each poem was incredibly descriptive but gave nothing away, unless someone who suspected Randal's telepathic dark powers read in between the lines.

From a literary point of view, it was outstanding. In an investigatory capacity, it revealed a hidden chain of events. It was like the poetical diary of a serial killer. It was all there, with intervals of unrelated pieces of work, designed to throw the reader off the true scent.

The poem 'Halloween Dream' was the longest in the book and Patrick felt it was a masterpiece of engineered distraction to encourage the reader to become so absorbed in its epic production, that they would not pay too much analytical heed to the rest. He would have to meet up with Leonard and plan their next move. He still strongly suspected Randal's telepathic involvement with past murders.

Randal courted publicity on his own terms. It was not as overdone as his publishers would have liked it to be but it aroused public interest because it gave him a slightly mysterious edge. It had mixed reactions in the literary circles.

"I think it's a bit self-indulgent. He reads like an old man with all his life behind him instead of ahead," drawled one critic.

"I disagree. I think it's a refreshing piece of self-examination. Very personal and yet candid in its approach. His words are sensational," argued another.

Whatever the opinion, it was the talk of the college and Randal Forbes became a name to note within its hallowed rooms. Many of the male students latched on to him, wanting to be his friend but he only chose the cream of the crop and rejected the others quite casually. Girls flocked around him in huge droves and he used their favours to boost his ego and widen his sexual leanings. It came with the territory and he milked it accordingly.

Clive had to deal with it all and say nothing.

So many intruders but all I can do is stay loose and watch the Beaumont back-slapping. It's just a rehearsal because widespread fame is on the cards. That's the trouble. He's not my possession, damn it. Everyone wants a piece of him. Anyone who can paint such incredible pictures in words should never be chained. He belongs to the world now. I'll have to psych myself into acceptance with respect to his power. Anyway, they can all kiss his feet a thousand times a day but they'll never get close. I've the monopoly on that one and they'll envy me. He's so damn hot it's a crime. I wish that was his only crime.

Clive sighed deeply. He lit up a cigarette as he contemplated the future; his and Randal's.

I'm in prime position. None of them know about 'the gift'. I'm the only one he's confided in. No matter how many people are to be told, if any at all, I'll always be at the front of a long queue of desperate followers, all dizzy with desire for his love and respect. So, all you sycophants, stand in line and don't hold your breath.

★★★

Patricia Forbes was now seventeen and in the lower-sixth of her grammar school, preparing for the build-up to her A-Level mocks. She was a popular pupil but now found herself even more so as Randal's sister. As much as she loved her brother, she was becoming tired of all the unknown faces swarming around her because of the connection. She was looking forward to a school trip abroad in the approaching spring, where she could practise her French, and rid herself of all the unwanted attention she was receiving.

Perhaps deep down she was a little miffed at his triumph and this annoyed her intensely because she had never felt jealous before of his genius and took pride in being his close family.

From his brief letters to her and his very fleeting return home last Christmas, it seemed that Randal was lording it over the inhabitants of Oxford. As usual, Clive was superglued to his side. Now she was older, she could see the complete and total power her brother had over his best friend.

On Boxing Day, Clive and his parents had called round for a seasonal drink to her house. She had wanted to show Randal a photograph of her beautiful French pen friend and walked in, quite innocently, on him and Clive in the bedroom. She stood frozen in the doorway as she saw them fondling each other.

"I love you," groaned Clive, as Randal's hands moved expertly over his private parts, in between heavy breathing.

"Do you now?" replied Randal in a thick voice, pressing himself up against Clive with urgent movements.

Patricia vacated the room and closed the door as quietly as possible. She would not have believed it, had she not seen it with her own eyes.

My God! Does Alison know? She can't do! She's desperately in love with Randal and I thought he was with her! I feel sorry for anyone who falls under his spell. Nobody's completely immune. Not even me! He uses that famous smile of his to get around me when I'm annoyed and strokes my face in a gesture of apology and I can't resist his charms. So, what chance would Alison or Clive have for that matter?

As shocked as she was, she still had to stifle a giggle at the thought of her father knowing the truth. Edward Forbes was a staunch example of the old boys' network and took immense satisfaction in his son's public standing.

He'd horsewhip the pair of them and send Clive on his merry way, head first through the nearest bloody window. Mum would burst into tears because her precious son had fallen heavily off his gilded pedestal, into the fires of hell. My lips are sealed.

Patricia was very broad-minded and certainly no prude but the discovery of her brother's bisexuality was quite an eye-opener.

He told me only recently that he intended to marry Alison when the time's right! Does he plan to ditch Clive's services before or after his marriage vows? Maybe he needs the pair of them to feed his androgynous appetite. This isn't frivolous and someone will get hurt in the end and I'll put money on it that it won't be my one and only decadent brother. For sure!

★★★

Marcus Pennington sat in the college's Hulme common room, which served as the centre of daily life for graduates. He sipped his coffee, engrossed in his reading matter. Marcus had borrowed Clive's copy of *Poetic Justice* and was about halfway through the book when he came upon the much-talked-about 'Halloween Dream', which was the inspiration to the new play Randal was writing, exclusively for The Beaumont Players, hopefully to be presented in the Trinity Term.

Against his hope of finding the work to be contrived and superficial, which was how he viewed its author, Marcus was more than impressed by its structure and composition, as he was drawn into Randal's irreverent world of demonism. The words danced on the paper in front of his eyes and he found himself going back to the first verse, to read it all again, regardless of its length and content.

> *I had a supernatural dream*
> *One windy night on Halloween*
> *When spirits danced on leaves of green*
> *With weeping willows in between*
> *And on the rustic moonlit lawn*
> *The elves and fairies stalled the dawn*
> *To watch the midnight magic spawn*
> *The witches in their robes reborn.*

Around the brown and spangled gold
As autumn shadows braced the cold
The warlocks' whispered manifold
Those spells they wove from scriptures old
And in the esoteric light
Where flights of fancy sparked the night
Bell book and candle fawned in sight
For witches bathed in ghostly white.

Above the cry of hooded crow
The sky of blackened indigo
Threw out a strange unearthly glow
To greet the chants of long ago
As shapes and cloaks swayed round the moon
In homage to symbolic rune
All phantom creatures rasped in tune
The witches own endemic croon.

The night embraced the witching hour
The woodland nymph began to cower
As wolf and wizard wielded power
On russet leaf and dying flower
The air hung heavy with the scent
Of witch's brew and mal-intent
As mantles flapped on figures bent
Who chanted spells intransigent.

Marcus licked his lips and flicked over the page to get to the next verse. The hairs on the back of his neck stood to poetical attention, and against all his resolve, he carried on reading, his love of English language being nurtured by Randal's unique, imaginative creativity.

The fireflies flickered fancy-free
In lines of perfect symmetry

In solace and affinity
As if to break the spell on me
All noble deeds were laid to rest
And banished to the wilderness
With pageantry of pagan dress
For sorcerer and sorceress.

The stars played tricks upon the eye
Like magic lanterns in the sky
Which, in turn, seemed to magnify
Reflected light both low and high
Like some demented violin
Each chant was music to the wind
Both black and white lived on therein
As likewise to a harlequin.

The night owl flinched to see them come
As forest life began to hum
And all was underneath the thumb
Of heresy and heathendom
Amidst the cackles and the cries
Long fingers curled to tantalise
And pointed hats could not disguise
The power of magnetic eyes.

I knew I could not break the spell
Of whispered word and bantam yell
No blarney stone or wishing well
Could free me from this haunted dell
A childish game of trick or treat
With witch's mask or ghostly sheet
Would fail immensely to compete
With all this magic under feet.

This panorama filled the night
Like summer skies with birds in flight
As paint on canvas craves the sight
Of perfect scenes Pre-Raphaelite
And as the mood intensified
All cowardice inside me died
As Mother Earth, arms open wide
Embraces sea and ebbing tide.

The wind whipped up the falling leaves
Whilst moon and sky were thick as thieves
And ravens clustered in the eaves
As offspring to each parent cleaves
The night took on a different slant
Mere mortal life seemed oddly scant
Mesmeric sounds in every chant
Unholy and yet sacrosanct.

Marcus felt his fingers tremble slightly as he turned the page to find out the writer's fate.

The nightlife scuttled all around
So finely tuned to every sound
Impatient to be homeward bound
And safe within their hallowed ground
My eyes were fixed in vacant stare
The cauldron hissed then stained the air
And time stood still as if to snare
All demonism living there.

A smell of incense filled my head.
It filtered through the forest bed
The mouse turned tail, the badger fled
Through bracken fields of damson red

I listened as the coven choir
Sang out with venomous desire
And felt a rush of ice and fire
Surge through my veins from out the mire.

I caught the flashing of a sword
Its scabbard scratched and slightly flawed
In ancient times it may have gored
Some medieval overlord
Its might was individual
With power quite residual
Its movement seemed habitual
No stranger to this ritual.

A golden goblet filled with wine
Was passed around from time to time
And all about me seemed to dine
On shades of hemlock and of pine
All creatures earthed or on the wing
Those insects drowsy or with sting
And each surrounding living thing
Consorted in a magic ring.

A force reached out as if to find
The darkest corners of my mind
Unleashing powers of its kind
All elements were intertwined
And like a comet lost in space
Which tries to find its rightful place
I parted from the human race
A pilgrim who had slipped from grace.

Marcus could totally understand why Clive was under Randal's spell as his eyes devoured the last few verses on the next page.

His hands shook but he could not put it down. He wanted to, but something was making him read on.

Something quite primeval.

I floated forward in a daze
Through black and silver timeless haze
To shadows cast in different greys
Through bodies banded in a maze
The air became as cold as ice
Its silence gripped me like a vice
It hungered for a sacrifice
Was I about to pay the price?

Then overhead I heard a crash
Of thunderclouds overtly brash
I saw the lightning's ugly gash
Cut through the sky with violent slash
And as all hell let loose and broke
With incantations to invoke
It all changed with one single stroke
And fell apart as I awoke.

I wallowed in the aftermath
Like soaking in a tainted bath
And in my head that pagan path
A paranormal photograph
Yet in the sunlight it would seem
Such forces are but unforeseen
And was it only just a dream
That windy night on Halloween?

Marcus felt the sweat on the sides of his brow start to run down his face and trickle around his jawline. Yesterday, he had watched Randal in action, holding court in the same room as he was now. He studied Clive's worshipping features as his icon gave his views on Middle English literature. If he did not know better, Marcus could believe that Randal had existed before, so vivid were his descriptions, but although he was deadly accurate quoting the poetry, Randal was derisive and disparaging about the poets. It was almost heretical as he appeared to derive great personal satisfaction from cutting the strong religious aspect down to some shrunken, meaningless condition of intellectual stagnation. Throughout the whole discussion Marcus had tried to remain objective and detached but he had found himself being dragged by his hair into Randal's circle of mass veneration.

It was those strange, animated, alien eyes that compelled him to listen and watch with bated breath. They spoke of something ethereal but unholy and he felt every pore of his skin stand up in response. Marcus's maternal grandfather was a priest who always looked for the good in his fellow man. He had argued with him many times about there being no heaven or hell, in the sense of existing above and below. He loved his grandfather but was at odds with him about religion and felt it would be hypocritical for him to attend church services just because he was related.

All this was true, but when Randal had turned to him unexpectedly in the middle of his blasphemous rhetoric, and fixed his slate-grey, yellow-glinting, glittering eyes on his own, suddenly every one of the sermons which he had been taught from the pulpit as a child seem to come to the aid.

Of all consecrated life.

★★★

Auditions were being held for Randal's play *Telesthesia* which had a supernatural theme; good against evil, with the power to predict. Randal was absolutely buzzing and The Beaumont Players were excited about the drama, especially in view of his current high profile. Randal had a large part in the production, both as an actor and director. The interviews were taking longer than he wished, but it was important to get it one hundred per cent right. True to form he had chosen to play the black angel but he needed someone to oppose his dark side. So far, he had not found him.

"Get me another coffee, Clive, please!" he ordered. "This is thirsty work."

"Anything else, your highness?" asked Clive in a deliberate Uriah Heap tone.

"This is going to be a long, long day," sighed Randal, too preoccupied to react to Clive's sarcasm.

An impressive figure walked into the room causing Randal to do a double-take. He looked the image of his young cousin, Dean Thornton.

Whoa! This is how Dean will look in seven years' time!

The likeness robbed Randal of his speech. Someone handed the student his script and he began reciting the lines. He was a good actor. It was very evident in his delivery. His jet-black hair shone under the lights and his bright blue eyes burned with holy passion.

Randal imagined him in full stage make-up. His skin would look even lighter under the greasepaint and his eyes could be emphasised to look more outstanding. He was tall and slim, with a striking posture and just the right amount of charm. He projected his words well, as his voice reached out towards the back of the room, without amplification. His wholesome looks and clean image would lend themselves beautifully to the character. He was so angelic that he had Randal looking for his wings, which would have irritated him beyond endurance under different circumstances.

I need this guy to play opposite me. He's perfect for the part.

Randal called him over and was even more amazed at his likeness to Dean.

"Would you like a coffee while we fill in the questionnaire?" asked Randal, getting up to shake his eager hand. He clasped Randal's firmly and smiled widely.

"Yes thanks, that'd be great. I hope you liked my audition," he enthused.

"Let's just go through the formalities and then we can get down to business, huh?"

"Of course."

Randal produced a sheet of paper to take down the particulars but inside he knew that he had found his sanctified opposition.

"Ok then, before we go any further, lets get acquainted. I'm Randal Forbes and you are… ?"

"The name's Sterling; John Robbie Sterling, but my friends all call me Robbie."

Randal froze. Time stood still and then spun backwards to the spring of 1965 when his unmarried and pregnant Aunty Dottie had appeared on his mother's doorstep, with dark circles under her pretty blue eyes. He could not believe this ironic twist of fate that stood before him in the shape of John Sterling's son, and Dean's half-brother. Had 'the gift' shaped this circumstance or was it just one of those uncanny events amidst the inescapable journey through life? For once Randal did not have the answer.

"Well then, Robbie, let's get down to business because you're more than suited to the part," confirmed Randal in a friendly voice, with no sign of the turmoil racing around in his head.

Robbie's smile stretched even wider across his face.

"Great!" he said punching the air with triumph. "I was hoping you'd say that. I've read your work and quite frankly I can't put your stuff down."

"Stuff?"

"Yeah, your poetry. It's brilliant!"

Randal's mouth curled slightly upwards with sick humour and contempt. He was sure that his new recruit would not be so ardent about his creations if he knew the real truth of the matter. He looked closely at the face opposite his own. Half of him warmed towards the features because they were so like Dean's but the other half felt a surge of pure hatred for the father who had created them.

"What are you studying?" asked Randal casually.

"Medicine. I'm in my second year."

"I see. So how did you hear about my play?"

"Are you kidding? It's the talk of the college. I'm greatly interested in the arts, especially dramatics. Taking part in this production is a source of relaxation. It takes me away from the pressures of my studies, if you get my drift."

"Drift noted. Are there any medics in your family? Your father perhaps?" pumped Randal with deliberate guile.

Robbie's eyes clouded over and he moistened his lips before answering.

"My father died when I was a child."

"I'm sorry to hear that. Is that why you want to be a doctor?"

"No. He wasn't ill… he was… he was… murdered. They never found his killer. It's taken me a long time to adjust but I've come to terms with it now. My mother hasn't. She's still affected," whispered Robbie.

"I see," replied Randal when he saw the shutters come down.

I see, you son-of-a-toerag. I don't know what I'm going to do with you after this.

Randal went through the motions of auditioning the last few students who were still waiting but he already had his main player. Robbie had the other major role. Randal was in full flow as he courted his theatrical side, hypnotising him with his vast command of prose and classical literature. Robbie could not believe the incredible amount of information that Randal had digested in the short time he had been at Beaumont and thought it was amazing.

He's a genius with a huge capacity for endless absorption.

Randal continued his journey into a literary past and Robbie felt that he was being sucked into a verbal cocoon of phonology. He looked deeply into the slate-grey irises and charcoal pupils of Randal's eyes, attracted by their yellow glints, which appeared almost amber in a certain light. He had never seen such unusual eyes. Nor had he ever met anyone like him before.

He's positively out of this world with a self-confidence and cognisance far beyond his years. He's a verbal wonderland of knowledge. I wish I'd met him years ago. I always wanted a brother. I'm sandwiched between two sisters. I was only eight when Dad was killed. Mum's never recovered and she's still a depressive. We've all suffered. Having a brother like Randal would have been so healing for me.

Robbie shook his head as if to rid himself of all the negative recollections. He thought he was over that painful analysis so why was he torturing himself now? He should be celebrating his success at landing an impressive part in Randal's play, not tormenting himself with yesterday's grief.

It was as if Randal's perception on life and death had kick-started a whirlpool of mental activity in his head and split his mind wide open, letting in the bad with the good.

A ripple of apprehension tingled along Robbie's spine and he wondered why. What was he worried about anyway? Randal Forbes or just the emotions he had invoked? He was a year older than Randal and presumably wiser. So why did he feel almost gauche and subordinate in his presence? It did not make any sense because Randal was going out of his way to be amiable and informative.

Randal knew exactly the effect he was having on his bewildered listener. He was working his black magic slowly and effectively upon his new acquaintance, confusing him with dramatic rhetoric as he cogitated. *I'm going to win you over, John*

Robbie Sterling, and you'll automatically take me into your misplaced confidence. I'm prickling with curiosity about your childhood and the other snivelling siblings at your sickening side. I've shaped their past and now destiny has delivered you into my arena.

"When do you think *Telesthesia* will be staged?" asked Robbie excitedly.

"In the Trinity Term hopefully; well that's the aim," replied Randal with a miniscule glint in his alien eyes.

"That's good; something to look forward to," smiled Robbie.

"Indeed. It's always good to have something to look forward to, especially with all the endless studying," smiled Randal, but inwardly he seethed. *Indeed, and it's only poetic justice to have a heinous hand in your future. Then terminate it.*

★★★

Rehearsals for *Telesthesia* began a fortnight after Randal's initial introduction to Robbie Sterling. It would be the major theatrical event of the year. Most of the former productions had been put on at different venues, such as the Frewin Gardens or the Playhouse. For the first time ever, Randal had been granted permission to use the College Hall. He had ingratiated himself with most of the academic, administrative and support staff, meeting the Vice Chancellor himself, who was usually way beyond any undergraduate's social, or indeed, academic sphere. Randal had already touched each and every one of their lives, partly through his new-found fame but mostly due to his devastating charm and intellect.

Clive would witness each run-through, happy to breathe the same air.

"You could have a part in it, you know. You've only got to say the word," encouraged Randal.

"No thanks. I'm just happy to observe the way it's all coming together and witness the enthusiasm of the players. I think they've become used to my non-contributory presence. Anyway, I'm finding my workload hard enough as it is. If I'm going to get anywhere with my exams then I need to study. It's crucial to my time at Beaumont because I've got to make sure I'm good enough to stay here for another two years. You're always ten moves ahead of me. You thrive on it all," smiled Clive.

When Clive first set eyes on the whole of the cast, his attention was immediately drawn to the tall, dark figure playing directly opposite Randal. He looked familiar but he could not put a name to his face. It was at the end of one particular rehearsal, when Randal introduced him to Robbie, that the big, shiny penny dropped.

Oh God! That name! John Sterling! Now it's all clicked into place. I worked out that you had a telepathic hand in his father's death. My head's whirling. What are you up to now? Is this some kind of continuous revenge cycle in which you're going to punish all John Sterling's offspring, except Dean?

Randal heard Clive's thoughts and laughed to himself. It amused him.

"I think we should go out for a drink tonight. What do you say, Robbie? Are you up for it? Let's get to know each other better," coaxed Randal.

"You bet I am and the first round's on me!"

"What about you, Clive? Are you coming with as well?" asked Randal.

"Well, OK then. I can't stay out too late though. I've got an early tutorial tomorrow."

They made their way to the students' bar and found a table. Clive had not eaten and did not want a repeat performance of the 'Alison evening' by drinking too much on an empty stomach. Besides, his insides were already in knots. Clive watched Randal's reactions closely as Robbie spoke animatedly about his life. He knew his lover only too well and saw his expression grow harder when Robbie mentioned his concern for his family. His heart skipped several beats as he caught the molten glitter in Randal's evil stare when Robbie touched upon his father's untimely death.

And Clive felt no jealousy over Randal's new friend; only pity for his latest unsuspecting victim.

3

Marcus had invited Clive for the weekend to his family ancestral home in Banbury, which was just outside Oxford. His parents, Lord and Lady Pennington, were prosperous landowners and had come into various properties through inherited wealth on his father's side. Home was Clarendon Hall, a sprawling estate of many acres. Marcus had an older sister, Felicity, who was married to a French barrister and lived abroad. His younger brother, Thomas, was still at boarding school and was also hoping to secure a place at Beaumont when the time came.

Clive was torn. Randal had decided on the spur to visit Stratford-upon-Avon at the same time and had encouraged Clive to join him, knowing he had been asked to meet Marcus's family. He wanted to see the Royal Shakespeare Company tread the boards and thought that Clive could easily visit Banbury another time. Randal knew that Marcus had become a good friend to Clive and that he was looking forward to meeting his parents and staying over at Clarendon.

As usual, Randal had succeeded in disturbing Clive's schedule. The thought of missing out on spending two days and nights in a creative and intimate atmosphere with him, threw Clive into an immediate dilemma over which invitation to accept. But that was Randal's intention anyway.

Marcus disliked Randal intensely. He loathed the way Clive was at his constant beck and call. Many times, he drew attention to the fact but could not shatter Clive's brick-hard wall of defensive loyalty.

"But he's a user! Can't you see that? He's being bloody selfish because he doesn't want you to spend the weekend with me!" snapped Marcus when he found out about Randal's last-minute invitation and Clive's apparent indecision.

"That's not true. You don't know him like I do. He loves me. He really does, but in his own way," insisted Clive, his words falling on deaf ears.

"Crap! Randal loves Randal."

"Don't talk about him like *that!* You're way out of line!"

"Look, Clive, the sooner you realise his shortcomings then the better for you, me and everyone else. Wake up to yourself. How long are you going to be his slave? Are you hanging around as background scenery all your life? Waiting for the few stale crumbs of affection he throws your way when he feels like it? And what about Alison? Are you going to be the first best man to kiss the bridegroom or are you planning to sleep between them on their fucking honeymoon?" cursed Marcus.

"Oh, shut up! Leave me alone! You don't understand! You'll never understand so just take a hike!" snapped Clive and stormed out of the room.

Marcus sat at the table with his head in his hands. *It had to be said*, he thought. Although only friendship had transpired between him and Clive, Marcus had fallen for him. Behind his jealous rage he had spoken the truth and Clive knew it. That is why he left the room in a strop. The truth always hurt.

But somehow Marcus felt that Randal would always escape its painful realisation.

Clive headed in the direction of Randal's room. All the way there Marcus's words were ringing in his head and making him depressed. Maybe it would serve Randal right if he refused to go with him but it would kill him to do so. Marcus could not begin to understand the reasons behind his allegiance to Randal because if he did, he would not mock it, or compare it to that of a vassal's fealty to his feudal lord. It was difficult to put his adoration into layman's terms.

What Marcus had said was partly true but he could not say to him that he felt chosen to protect the receiver of 'the gift'. His love for Randal was so vast, it was almost cosmic in proportion and the physical side was only a part of the whole. Marcus had hit upon mere mortal observation, which was hard enough to bear without outside interference.

Clive knocked on Randal's door. He was already expecting him and opened it with a smile, as he let him in.

"Hello you. What's new?" inquired Randal, pulling his black sweater over his head.

"Oh, nothing much. Just the usual, you know," replied Clive, sitting on the bed and kicking off his sandals, his heart doing the usual flip at Randal's suffocating, seductive presence.

He stretched out full length on the mattress and caught a glimpse of bare chest as Randal slipped into his top.

"Fancy a drink with a couple of the Beaumonts?" asked Randal, referring to the cast in his play.

"Where?"

"We thought we'd go to the Head of the River. It's a nice night to get stoned. Come on, Clive, lose that hangdog look and just lighten up. Hmm?"

"I'm not sure. You don't need me with all your fellow thespians in tow and I'm not in the mood for any in-depth analysis. All they talk about is Chaucer, Dryden and Browning and that's before the first drink."

Randal laughed and Clive swooned.

He looks so dynamic. Six foot two inches of seductive manhood dressed in black. I'll never get tired of him. Marcus pales into insignificance. I'm hooked. Lost.

Randal heard Clive's thoughts and his expression softened.

"Come with, that's why I'm taking them all to the pub, so they can get blotto and forget to talk shop," he smiled.

"I need to talk to you about this weekend."

"What about it?" asked Randal, making his way over to the sink to wash his face.

"Marcus invited me to his place first. If I go to Stratford with you, I'll let him down. I'd rather be with you but I don't want to upset his plans. You understand. Don't you?"

Randal rinsed the soap off with a cold-water flannel. He reached out slowly for the hand towel to dry himself with over-elaborate movements, meticulously designed to enhance Clive's discomfort. He sat on the edge of the bed, looking at Clive with an expression of bored piquancy.

"Understand what?" he drawled. "I would have thought that the gates of Clarendon would be open to you another time. Or are you very anxious to consummate your relationship with its son and heir in the privacy of his noble, aristocratic walls?"

Clive blushed. As far as he was concerned it was not the uppermost thing in his mind but he knew it was definitely top of the agenda for Marcus. However, he was delighted with the reaction it had provoked in Randal. Could it be that he was actually jealous? Well, it would do him no harm to be on the redundant side of the fence for a change.

"Does it bother you?" asked Clive straight out with new-found confidence.

"Yup."

"Oh," was all Clive could say as they looked at each other intently.

Randal knew that Clive would never betray his trust. He was not the problem but Marcus Pennington was. Every time their paths crossed, Randal caught Marcus looking at him with a disdainful, probing expression, as if he was trying to infiltrate his thoughts but was annoyed with himself for bothering. On top of his suspicion, the man was insanely jealous of his relationship with Clive. His animosity was very transparent and Randal felt he could prove to be a meddlesome rival.

He needed to win him over and the only way would be in a one-to-one situation outside of the college. An idea was quickly formulating in Randal's head. He would let Clive believe that he was hurt by his preference to stay at Clarendon and would play on his conscience to that effect.

"I really, really wanted us to be together but, well, I don't wish to crowd your space," appealed Randal to Clive's soft nature.

"I prefer to be with you. You know I do but Marcus asked me first and it's only right that…"

"It's OK. It's all OK," interrupted Randal. "You go and do your own thing. I understand but I just wish… oh never mind."

"Wish what?"

"Well, to tell you the truth, I just wish that Marcus didn't have such a downer on me. He's always jumping to conclusions and wrong ideas about my intentions. I'm glad he's your friend because we all need other people. I'd really like to get to know him better but he won't give me a chance. Do you think you could make it right?" inquired Randal deceptively.

"He doesn't know you. He only thinks he does."

"So, help me prove him wrong. Let's all be friends and ditch the bad vibes."

A knock at the door ambushed their conversation at a vital point.

"Who the hell's this now? My room's been like a train station today."

Robbie Sterling stood there with a wide smile, holding the script to Randal's play under his arm.

"Hey! How you doing? I won't keep you a minute, it's just something I need to go over with you," he said cheerfully.

Robbie looked across at the bed and saw Clive reclining. He put a wrong interpretation on the situation.

"Sorry," he said, "when's the best time?"

"You can see him now if you like. I've gotta go," said Clive as he stood up, brushing bits of fluff off his jeans. "Nothing personal, Robbie, I've an important tutorial in fifteen minutes."

"Maybe we could get together again one evening? All three of us I mean; like last time?"

"Sure, why not?" replied Clive. "I'll talk to Marcus," he whispered into Randal's ear as he brushed past him and left.

Robbie immediately began to explain his uncertainties as to his ability to act out some of the more abstract scenes and there followed a long discussion on the true essence of their contents. Randal made a great pretence of appreciating Robbie's opinions on his work but deep down he was seething with well-hidden contempt, even though some of the observations were valid.

He studied his mannerisms through a narrow gaze and realised just how much of his son-of-a-bitch father was actually in him. The bile rose up in the back of his throat and he struggled to control the escalating stirrings of 'the gift' because he knew it would show in his eyes. The enormity of the whole situation hit him hard.

What the hell am I playing at? Encouraging Dean's half-brother to step so casually into my inner circle? At first it seemed incredibly fated but now the novelty is wearing very, very thin.

There was always someone spoiling the perfection. Everything was going so well until Marcus Pennington and Robbie Sterling had stepped into the arena. Something had to be done about them both. Robbie was already a follower but a marked man because of his paternal connection. He would be dealt with when the time was right. In the Randal way.

Marcus was not so easy. A fractured peace existed between them, solely due to their mutual respect for Clive. It was imperative for Randal to gain Marcus's confidence, respect and total acceptance in order to eradicate any conspicuous hostility between them.

That way if any harm should befall him, Randal would not be remotely connected or associated with his demise.

Marcus had requested to see the script to *Telesthesia* and Clive had managed to obtain a copy for his perusal. Against his better wishes, he found himself once more being drawn into the dark, mysterious literary world of Randal Forbes. There was no doubt that it was beautifully written; ingenious, in fact, beyond the scope of normal perception, through its classical journey into the unknown. The play only added to the mixed feelings that he had about its author and the contents left him in a conflicting state of equanimity and chaos. If only he could put his finger on the source of all the confusion. Randal's popularity was a thorn in his side because right from the beginning he had made his mind up to dislike him and the mere mention of his name started a chain reaction of negative thoughts.

Why has he such an effect on me? I loathe his hold over Clive but even that doesn't justify my bias and deep mistrust. No! It's something much more. There's an aura of dark evangelism around him. He's a fallen angel preaching defective propaganda to his flock. A demonic pulse is in his work. The written word reaches out to the reader, snaking into the subconscious and leaving its blemish. Am I the only one who suspects something or is there anybody else out there with similar qualms? There's no point in asking Clive. He's like a besotted manservant and always on the defensive when I try to discuss the matter. I'm positive he's hiding something and lives in fear of the revelation.

Marcus's maternal grandfather, the Right Reverend Leslie Stainthorpe, still had authority over his own parish and was nearing his retirement. He intended to remain in the village and live out the rest of his life surrounded by his family and friends, in a nearby country house, close to the church. Marcus was sure that his grandfather had a 'nose' for sensing anything or anyone who was connected with the dark side. They still differed over their opinion on the origin of such a force but they both believed it existed in some form or other.

The only way he could get them to meet would be to invite Randal down, with Clive, to Clarendon Hall. He would have to be very careful about the way he phrased the invitation. It was important to make the offer of hospitality look as genuine as possible.

Marcus decided to have a talk with his grandfather beforehand and put him in the suspicious picture. He would try to explain his mistrust without sounding irrational. He had to work out a precise plan of action and felt greatly comforted by his mental decision to act quickly upon such a strategy.

His attention was drawn back to the script in his possession. He had not finished reading it all and was curious as to the conclusion of the play. As he perused the lines, the paper seemed to grow hot in his hands. He looked down in disbelief as the words began to glow in front of his eyes.

What the hell's happening here?

His fingertips felt scorched and he gave a sharp intake of breath as he tossed the manuscript to the floor. It was a warm day but the room felt suddenly cold and he shivered as he stepped over the discarded pages on the ground. Either it was a psychological reaction to all his probing or he was up against a powerful, impious energy that knew no bounds.

And Marcus had the immovable feeling it was more so the latter of the two theories.

★★★

Randal heard from Alison on the same day that Marcus had invited him to Clarendon Hall, for the weekend, with Clive.

When Randal asked Marcus if he could bring her along, he was told that she would be most welcome and that his family were great admirers of her musical talent. Secretly Marcus was enormously relieved that she would be coming because Randal would be less aware of any close scrutiny.

Clive was unsure about the whole thing, especially when he heard that Alison would put in a personal appearance.

His head spun with the familiar whirling sensation of stress and anxiety over Randal's movements. Firstly, he could not understand why Randal was so keen on changing Marcus's low opinion of him. When Randal had wanted Clive to "make it right" it did not ring true.

Secondly, Marcus had miraculously invited Randal before Clive had actually buttered him up in the hope of such an invitation. Randal was delighted and immediately dropped all his plans to visit Stratford-upon-Avon. Remarkably, Marcus was very pleased he had done so. Why the sudden turn around on both sides to kiss and make up? It was all so odd.

Clive was lost in thought. *I feel like an uninformed pawn in a clandestine liaison. I've gone over it all trying to make sense of the whole arrangement but I can't come up with an answer. Perhaps they really want a harmonious atmosphere because I'm involved. Maybe Randal's trying his best to form some kind of peace treaty with Marcus and vice versa. Could it really be that simple? They both seem happy at the idea of spending time with each other and Marcus is definitely looking forward to seeing Alison. Even though I'm not. God it's complicated.*

Clive prayed that they would all have their own rooms. Even though he knew that Randal would somehow find his way to Alison's bed, he would be fractionally comforted by the fact that they would at least begin the night separately.

Marcus is going to make a pass at me. I know it. It's been on the cards for some time now. Clarendon's a sprawling Estate and separate bedrooms are no problem. I've got visions of all the doors opening in the dead of the night and the four of us colliding into each other on some creaking landing, evoking disapproving glances from the portraits of the Pennington lineage. I've got to laugh at that. Anyway, this is all conjecture. I'm driving myself mad. Again! Building up a warped scenario out of my distorted thoughts.

On the Friday evening before the weekend in question, Clive had looked astonished when Randal asked Marcus to join them.

"Here's to you, Master Pennington, and thanks for the invitation; it's much appreciated," gushed Randal, holding up his glass of wine in a friendly toast, brilliantly disguising his intense dislike of his host.

"My pleasure. My family are all looking forward to meeting you, and Alison of course. They're fans of her music," replied Marcus, blanking out unrighteous thoughts.

Had Clive been aware of their exact intentions towards each other, he would have kissed goodbye to Clarendon Hall, begged Randal to do the same, and put an abrupt end to his blossoming friendship with Marcus.

★★★

Alison yawned and stretched out full length on her large, squashy leather settee. She was pleased with herself and her life. Tomorrow she would be seeing Randal again, even if she had to share him with other people. Her invitation to Clarendon was unexpected and would prove to be very interesting but as long as she was with Randal, anywhere would be exciting.

She had been busy of late, performing at various venues and concentrating on a new original piano piece.

She had sent Randal a demo tape of the composition for his opinion and he had written back immediately, encouraging her to put the final touches to another masterpiece. She was so in love with him it hurt. Everything she wrote was with him in mind and her imagination was permanently fired by the emotion he had awoken in her. Their coming together had left her on a creative high, wanting to express her passion in musical form.

He was always in her head but this did not distract her from her work. It heightened it. She had called her latest piece *Miracles* and it was her best work to date. Now that Randal had put his seal of approval on its birth, she would press forward with wild enthusiasm.

She had his photograph in her hand and began to trace her finger around the outline of his handsome face. She moved it closer to her lips and kissed the glass that covered his mouth, wishing it was the real thing and not some smiling image in a frame. She imagined him caressing her and a shiver travelled down the whole length of her spine. Her body started to ache for his touch and her skin felt hot in anticipation. She spoke his name out loud and held his picture to her breast as she closed her eyes.

The shrill ringing of the telephone brought her down to earth with a bump, as she reluctantly abandoned her sexual reverie. She glanced over at the clock and saw it was nearly midnight. For a moment she felt a ripple of alarm when she realised how late it was for someone to be calling her and hoped there was nothing wrong. She picked up the phone and put it to her ear.

"I can't stop thinking about you," murmured Randal before she even said 'hello'.

Alison's heart began thumping the second she heard his voice.

"Randal," was all she could say in response. The air crackled between them and her mouth felt parched.

"Alison, Alison," he whispered low. "I'm aching for you and I know you feel the same."

Her pulse became rapid and she felt unnerved by his uncanny accuracy. She instinctively knew that it was no coincidence he had phoned her. He had tuned in to her wavelength, as per usual.

The telepathic link frightened her, but excited her at the same time. It was getting stronger as though he was inside her head, probing her most secret thoughts and desires. She blushed like a virgin bride at the images of naked lust that filtered through her brain, sparked by the suggestive tone in his cultured, sexy voice. No other man had ever made her feel so wanton.

Randal laughed a deep, husky, knowing sound, as if he had glimpsed her erotic vision and thoroughly approved of its visual effects.

"You scare me," she said in a small voice, that she managed to dredge up from somewhere at the back of her closed throat.

"Do I now? Why?"

"Because," she responded ineffectively.

"That bad, huh?" he teased mercilessly and laughed once more.

Quite suddenly Alison had the strangest sensation that her very soul was being laid bare. It was as if he held the whole reason for her living right in the palm of his shapely hand. It made her feel powerless and vulnerable. She resented the feeling because she wanted to be his equal and not some impuissant marionette. She said nothing and the silence stretched across the airwaves between them.

"I love you," he said out of nowhere, as if to reassure her of her worth.

"I love you, too," she replied automatically because it was true.

"Love is always complicated so don't analyse it too much."

There! He had done it again! He had reached inside her head without any trouble at all, answering and advising her. She had always found this side of him disconcerting because it seemed stronger than just the usual telepathic link that often resides within a close relationship.

This was far more than that situation.

Alison had always been drawn to the spiritual. Being an artist, her mind was permanently open to the paranormal. She would soak up the influences and feed them all into her music, creating a distinctive sound for both herself and her audience. She sensed within Randal a veritable link with the unknown. She had always felt it but it grew stronger with each meeting. It was not only inside him but all around him. He throbbed with its force, affecting everyone and everything in his path. It was more than just a disturbance. She could only guess at the extent of his power. She did not associate it with anything dark. She did not have a clue to his satanic disposition. And she never would.

"Alison, come back to me," coaxed Randal softly. "I need to hear your voice before I go to bed."

"I'm still here. What do you want me to say?" she replied huskily.

Randal's voice was like a caress as he told her what he would like to hear. She responded to his instructions and her whole body became a mass of sensation as he verbally made love to her over the phone.

By the time she replaced the receiver she felt drugged and breathless. She fell into a deep satisfied sleep, knowing that the morning light would bring him back into her world for another weekend of cataclysmic passion.

★★★

Marcus's car screeched round the bend of the narrow country lane which would eventually lead to the main gates of Clarendon Hall. Alison laughed with Randal on the back seat, as the sudden movement jerked her into his arms. He whispered suggestively in her ear and she blushed, which amused him all the more. Marcus caught her red cheeks through his mirror and cringed at the effect. He could see that she was totally and utterly under the spell of his number-one foe.

Clive was also inescapably aware of the activity behind him. He had tried hard to relax in the front seat next to Marcus but had failed miserably in his attempt. Somehow his range of senses seemed to be fixed on the two voices behind him and nothing else.

Randal's first glimpse of the Pennington Estate and its ten acres of ground corresponded exactly to the vision he had plucked out of Marcus's head. His family had owned the property since medieval times and the Hall was now a good example of Victorian Jacobean style, with superb panelling and historic family furniture and paintings.

As the four of them approached the entrance hall with their overnight bags, Marcus explained that it differed from the original and that at some time in the nineteenth century, the east wall was opened up and the hall thrown open towards the elegant wooden staircase, which was now hung with a remarkable series of family portraits, in between eighteenth-century lamp brackets.

An elegantly dressed middle-aged man strode across to greet them and Marcus introduced him as Adams, who immediately offered his assistance. He had been a personal valet to Lord Pennington and also chief manservant of the household for the last ten years. He was instructed to show the guests to their rooms and then escort them to the parlour, where the rest of Marcus's family would be waiting for them to have lunch.

Clive had the sudden urge to laugh at the formality of it all, especially when he compared the butler's immaculate pinstriped trousers with Marcus's tatty denim jeans, covered in splodges of yellow poster paint, from an experimental mural he had attempted in his spare time, under the influence of vodka.

Adams told them all to leave their luggage as he would attend to it but they decided to take up their own cases. Clive had to stifle another chuckle when he saw that he thoroughly disapproved of their self-sufficiency and gave a stiff nod of his head in their direction, as if to prove the point.

"After we've all eaten, I'll show you around the Hall," confirmed Marcus, as they climbed the impressive staircase.

"Hmm," murmured Randal distractedly, as he felt the usual various invisible influences around him, which always resided in a place of historical value. He stiffened suddenly, as the ghosts of the past moved through his mind and body.

As they reached the landing, Marcus caught a strange flicker in Randal's alien eyes. The expression in them was decidedly macabre.

An icy hand seemed to leave its imprint around his throat and Marcus felt he was stepping right into the centre of the devil's playground.

As if to confirm his suspicion, Randal turned to look at him and although the eye contact could not have been more than a few moments, Marcus felt as if he was being superhumanly examined and dissected. Randal could smell his fear as sharply as a predatory animal could sniff out the cowardly scent of its prey.

"This way if you please," intervened Adams, as he urged Randal to follow him to his room.

The spell was broken by the butler's instructions but the episode was totally misinterpreted by Clive. All he saw was the visual exchange between Randal and Marcus and he jumped to his own painful, but erroneous, conclusion. Clive felt his stomach turn over as he presumed the worst.

Oh my God! Marcus has the hots for Randal and it's not one-sided! No wonder they were both eager to smoke their unexpected pipe of peace!

Clive's face looked grim as he watched Marcus make his way to his own room, leaving Adams in total charge of his guests.

Alison on the other hand was in her element. She always glittered amongst beautiful surroundings and felt well equipped to cope with her stay. Randal's wild lovemaking would be the icing on her extramarital cake and to hell with the consequences. She had worked incredibly hard on her music and was hungry for this exciting break in her hectic schedule.

She was in Miss Felicity's Room, as it was known when Marcus's sister used to live at home. This had originally been two rooms in the seventeenth century and one of the original windows had been blocked by the insertion of a cupboard. She walked over to study a series of delicate watercolours of the surrounding countryside, painted by a gifted family friend.

She sat down and ran her shapely fingers over the green Victorian bedstead, which was hung with glazed cotton chintz. She knew that Randal was in the room next door. There was only a wall separating them and her heart skipped several beats at the thought of the approaching night. She looked at her watch and saw it was just after twelve noon. Adams said he would call back for her in one hour's time, so she unpacked her clothes and freshened up for lunch.

Randal looked around his room after Adams had closed the door. He was in the 'blue bedroom' which was dominated by a mahogany four-poster bed. The bedhead, valances and footboard incorporated the Pennington coat of arms. The blue silk embroidered bedspread was the work of Marcus's great-grandmother.

The panelling of the room was grained to imitate cedar wood and a seventeenth-century Flemish tapestry draped the north wall. There was a small attractive dressing room leading off to the left, which contained an early shower bath. The windows overlooked the flower gardens and Randal feasted his eyes on the landscape below.

In his tasteful bedroom, Clive was not remotely interested in the grandeur of the house. He was deeply disturbed and emotionally agitated by his recent discovery and needed to speak to Randal urgently.

What the hell's going on here? What the fuck are you up to, Randal? I need to know!

A knock on each of their doors told them that their hosts were ready to receive them. Adams guided them to the Pennington's private parlour, whose rooms formed a family suite along the length of the west side of the house. Marcus had already gone on ahead to make sure that everything was in order but mostly to check if his grandfather had arrived. When he saw him sitting quite comfortably at the long mahogany table, he breathed a huge sigh of relief that his plan was now well and truly implemented.

Clive had decided to play his cards close to his chest and observe Randal and Marcus more closely before any accusations.

Surely Randal would not have brought Alison with him if he intended to amuse himself with Marcus? No way! I'm mistaken but was what that 'look' between them on the stairs? There must be another explanation. Here we go again; more insecurity and doubt over Randal's motives.

Marcus was waiting to present them to his family, and one by one, he made the introductions, starting with his mother, Fiona. The atmosphere was informal, which was the way she preferred it when her children's friends came to stay. Randal was instantly impressed by her beauty. She was smallish with long, dark hair which had been skilfully shaped into a chignon, revealing a slender, graceful neck adorned with a black velvet choker, which boasted a beautiful cameo brooch in the centre.

Her warm brown eyes were almond-shaped and when she looked downward, her eyelashes swept along the top of her high cheekbones. Her nose was dainty with a slight tilt at the tip. Her mouth was small but perfectly shaped and appeared coquettish when the corners turned upwards in a half-smile. She wore a simple white blouse inside a classically cut black skirt, which emphasised her slender curves. She looked altogether the prototype Lady of the manor.

Miles Pennington was quite tall with fair hair and twinkling blue eyes. His nose was slightly aquiline and his mouth generous. He sported the same gap in between his two front teeth as Marcus. He had a military bearing and exuded that natural indisputable confidence that belonged to the landed gentry.

"Hello, how lovely to meet you all. I'm so very pleased you could come," said Fiona in a lilting, cultured voice.

"The pleasure is all ours," replied Randal with his special, heart-stopping smile, as he picked up her hand and kissed it gently in an old-fashioned manner.

Fiona's heart fluttered unexpectedly. *Is this Clive? Marcus has spoken about him such a lot. He's so handsome and charming.* Randal heard her thoughts and cleared up the misunderstanding.

"I'm Randal Forbes. Clive's the one with the thatched halo of ginger hair and the eternal freckles," he joked but Clive was not amused.

"Well, hello Randal, and you too, Clive. Welcome to Clarendon Hall. Please, do sit down. Marcus has told me so much about you and his life at Beaumont College."

Randal smiled to himself at her initial mistake but his good humour evaporated instantly when Marcus introduced his grandfather, complete with dog collar and Bible.

The Right Reverend Leslie Stainthorpe had lived all his life in the sanctified shadow of the church. His wife had passed away one year ago, which had thrown a dark cloud over his impending retirement. His only daughter, Fiona, kept insisting that he come to live at Clarendon but he preferred his independence. Since his wife's death, his faith had strengthened and sustained him. Although he was seventy, he looked much younger and was very spritely. He had thick, strong, silver-grey hair and warm brown eyes which softened kindly when they alighted on his parishioners, especially those with a family problem or dilemma. He was thin but wiry and looked far taller than five feet ten inches in his priestly garb, delivering thought-provoking sermons from his pulpit.

Over the years he had encountered many different opinions. He had discussed his faith with atheists and agnostics. He lectured on the dangers of impiousness, profanity and irreverence. Through his experiences, he realised that he had a 'nose' for sensing an aura of evil around, or within, a person of lesser belief. It was as if these people were tottering on some kind of defective wavelength that he could sense and intercept.

He triumphed with some and others he lost, but had the satisfaction of knowing he had tried to save them. He always welcomed defiance if confronted with a non-believer and when Marcus had approached him with suspicion about a satanic newcomer in his academic circle, Leslie's curiosity was amplified due to his grandson's alarm and concern. He had never seen Marcus so disturbed. He was perpetually nervous, on edge and agitated.

Most of the time Marcus did his own thing and rarely came home. His mother had a good idea that her eldest son was not a lady-killer. The rest of the Pennington's were in the dark about his personal life and that was the way he preferred it to be. There were no questions asked, so no answers were required.

Leslie was very curious about Marcus's unwanted guest. He had read *Poetic Justice* right through from the start to the finish, to try and form some kind of picture in his mind of the author. There was no doubt that he was phenomenally gifted with a dark perception. So, by the time the weekend arrived, Leslie thought he was totally prepared and ready to receive him.

The introductions were nearly over and then Marcus led Randal to his grandfather, last of all. Leslie had been averting his eyes until that moment but now he looked up slowly, holding out his hand in hospitality.

"So nice to meet you," he said politely.

"The pleasure is all mine," drawled Randal, but inside he was furious.

Randal shook Leslie's hand. His touch was cold and clammy but that was not the undoing of the Reverend's soul.

It was those unreadable, piercing, infernal eyes that seared through his line of vision, right into the innermost depths of his being, and threw down their evil gauntlet in a monstrous challenge.

And for the first time ever, in the whole of his life, Leslie felt unaccountably ill-equipped to respond.

Leslie forgot to breathe. He knew that Randal could read his thoughts and would not let go of his hand. It was like a scene in a play where the two central characters had come together in a crucial place and their audience was waiting with bated breath for the outcome. Their eyes super-locked together and Leslie felt as if he was falling into a fathomless abyss, hurtling towards a situation he had only speculated about in a religious discussion, but had never experienced first hand.

The intense look between them provided the answer to both Marcus's and Clive's suspicions. Firstly, Marcus was totally convinced that he was justified with respect to his fears about Randal's satanic status. Secondly, Clive recognised the same visual exchange between Randal and the Reverend that had previously occurred on the staircase with Marcus, which he had mistaken for physical attraction. Clive realised that it was nothing to do with sexual chemistry but more in the way of a fearful recognition of something primeval, resulting in the immobilisation of eye contact. A huge weight lifted off his shoulders only to be immediately replaced by an uneasy apprehension as to Marcus's real motive in inviting Randal to his home. Clive felt tense.

Oh God. Look at the expression in Randal's eyes. He's livid. He's out for revenge.

Leslie felt Randal's fingers slide slowly through his own and release their clammy touch. His eyes were misty and he could hear the heavy thump of his heartbeat, pumping his lifeblood round and round his body at three times the normal speed. He sank back into his chair, struggling to gain his equilibrium and composure.

"Are you all right, Daddy? You look awfully pale," observed Fiona.

"Yes, yes, I'm fine; just a little overcome," Leslie forced himself to answer but he heard the tremor in his own voice.

Marcus bent down and put a reassuring arm around his grandfather's shoulder.

"Are you sure you're OK?" he added as he saw the ghastly pallor of Leslie's complexion.

"Don't fuss," whispered the Reverend and looked up at his grandson with a pleading expression to let the incident pass.

"May I help?" inquired Randal in a deceptively gentle voice, which sounded more like a deadly threat to Leslie's ears than a polite offer of assistance.

Marcus shook his head but kept his eyes averted away from Randal's gaze.

"I think I'll have a glass of port. That might bring my colour back," suggested Leslie in a breathless and uneasy tone.

"Not such a good idea if you don't mind me saying. It'll make you even more unsteady," advised Randal with glittering eyes.

The Reverend nodded in agreement; anything to stop Randal talking to him.

Things settled down and everyone took their places at the table for lunch and although Randal looked calm on the surface, a fire was blazing within him at the deception and treachery of his host's invitation.

Lunch was an introductory exercise and rather short-lived due to Marcus's impatience to show his guests around the Estate but more so to relieve his grandfather of Randal's presence. Alison was totally unaware of any adverse atmospherics within the company around her and was thoroughly enjoying her meal and the conversation throughout.

Randal gave no outward indication of any ill feeling and purposefully set out to bedazzle the Pennington clan with his own special brand of magical allure. Marcus observed in silent awe and dread the powerful impact that Randal was having upon his family, in both an exhilarating and debilitating sense. It was an unbelievable performance and he was torn between feelings of admiration and repugnancy at the effect.

"I'm sorry, Mother, for dragging them away, but they're really looking forward to a guided tour around the Hall," urged Marcus.

"Perfectly understandable. We can continue the conversation over dinner," she replied courteously.

As they left, Randal turned and gave her a dazzling smile. He knew that she was already hooked on his magnetism. If Marcus and the old priest wanted to play dangerous games, he could also join in and give them a mammoth run for their money.

"What a delightful young man," said Fiona to her husband Miles. "Did Marcus say that he's closer to Clive and that Randal is just an acquaintance? Pity. Clive seemed so introverted and ordinary in comparison."

"I agree but you know that Clive's parents are Paul and Rosemary Hargreaves, the famous novelists, don't you?" replied Miles in his defence.

"Yes, so they are. Alison's such a beautiful girl. She and Randal make a stunning couple. I must talk to her tonight about her music. She's very gifted," continued Fiona enthusiastically, dismissing Clive as background scenery.

"Would you excuse me please; I'm going to have a lie down," interrupted her father, getting to his feet slowly. "I just feel a tad tired."

"I'll see you upstairs, Daddy. You still look awfully pale to me," frowned Fiona.

"No, I'm fine; nothing that a short nap won't cure. See you later on and thank you for a lovely lunch."

The Reverend was desperate to be on his own and think things over. His head was whirling with theories and he had to organise his thoughts and decide on how he was going to deal with this unhallowed situation under his daughter's roof.

The afternoon sun was shining through his window so he closed the curtains to shut out the light. He drew on his inner strength as a man of the cloth. There was no doubt this was a first. He had felt a powerhouse of evil in Randal's gaze.

The boy has drained me with just one look. I can only guess at the potential of its full demonic force.

4

As Marcus showed them around the Hall, explaining the significance of each room and its artefacts, Clive was relieved to be away from the Reverend's extreme reaction to Randal. He wanted to ask Marcus point-blank what he was playing at and try to warn him off, without giving too much away. How he was going to stop Randal from retaliating was another problem.

Clive noticed that Marcus was avoiding Randal's eyes. When he asked him about the origin of the tapestries, Marcus replied to the walls, still shunning his gaze. As they viewed the library, Alison asked why there were pleated silk screens across the books and this time it was Randal who told her.

"It's a protection against fading, apparently a common nineteenth-century practice. Also, the furniture is late eighteenth- and early nineteenth-century, and the brass grate is Regency. The clock is nineteenth-century mother-of-pearl. I'm right. Aren't I, Marcus?" he asked in a silky-smooth, knowing voice.

"Yes," replied Marcus, still looking away.

"And, if I'm not mistaken, the tiles in the fireplace are of Dutch origin?"

Every muscle in Marcus's body seemed to stiffen in response to Randal's accuracy. He felt this unfamiliar sensation in his brain, as if an alien presence was scratching around inside, pulling at the cells and poaching information. For the first time in one hour, he turned around to actually look into Randal's eyes but there was nothing ominous there, and to all intents and purposes, Randal looked interested in the decorative workmanship of the room.

"Well? Are they?" reiterated Randal, pointing his hand in the direction of the tiles.

"Oh, the tiles; yes, they're Dutch," confirmed Marcus.

Alison linked her arm through Randal's and flattered him on his antiquarian knowledge.

Marcus could not prove it but felt sure that Randal was inside his head, picking his brains about the history of the Hall. He became even more convinced of his theory by the minute, as Randal continued to impress with his 'expertise' as they moved from room to room.

Presently they made their way to the gardens with its double herbaceous border and a unique clipped ilex avenue. They could not fail to be affected by the yew hedges and shrub rose collection. Nearby, there was a woodland walk and grove with rhododendrons, exotic shrubs and azaleas. Randal felt it was the most tranquil setting he had ever visited. Ghosts did not live here. Serenity and affinity fused together perfectly to create the ideal haven for a creative mind. He could easily unwind in its seclusion and take an occasional rest from 'the gift'.

He would work his magic all over Lord and Lady Pennington, which would ensure him a return visit. Randal smirked to himself. After all, this would be the perfect place to recharge his batteries once he had dealt with the old priest and his meddlesome grandson.

Evening found them all sat around the dinner table, which comprised of a suite of mahogany furniture, including fourteen dining room chairs with a broad moulded top rail, the legs nicely carved and reeded. The walls were full of family portraits and the room boasted a marble chimneypiece with an inset overmantel mirror. The mahogany-grained floor was a rare early nineteenth-century feature, and above the sideboard, in the area beyond the colonnade, hung a magnificent painting of the Hall, signed and dated 1834. The steps from the window to the left of the sideboard led into the walled flower garden.

Lady Pennington was hypnotised by Randal. She was completely entranced by his amazing knowledge and physical attributes. She sat wide-eyed and transfixed, watching him closely as he spoke, feeling the full impact of his dynamism.

Her father had spent most of the afternoon lying down, harnessing any reserve energy for the coming evening, in order to cope with his grandson's demonic guest, and sat through most of the meal, blanking out any adverse thoughts for fear of Randal picking up on them. Marcus felt like he was on trial and awaiting the verdict.

Alison spoke about her career and her hopes for the future but she too was under the spell of her vigorous lover.

Clive's head was full of unanswered questions which were causing him concern. He needed to get Randal on his own to discuss Marcus's folly but knew there was little chance of that, with Alison hanging on to his every word. Later, there would be even less opportunity, as she would be panting to get him under her sheets. It seemed to him that he lived his life walking on thin ice, over Randal-spawned situations. Sometimes the responsibility was just too much to bear and he wanted to break free. Once or twice he had been near to doing so, but then Randal would put a protective arm around his shoulder and he would melt, forgetting all prior uncertainties. Besides, he loved him deeply.

He watched the reaction to Randal's magnetism closely. He was a first-class operator and the Lady of the Hall was well and truly sucked in. Clive felt annoyed that he could not relax and show Marcus's mother his own intelligent and zany personality.

He felt as if he was letting Marcus down, because after all, he was his close friend, and Randal was just an associate.

All things considered, that was perhaps irrelevant. The main worry was Randal's reaction to the deception around him. Clive recognised the signs. It was the 'iron fist in the velvet glove' approach and he was buttering them all up before the kill.

Clive knew there would be a dramatic build-up to his vengeance and it would not take place overnight, so he still had time to talk Randal out of any malicious retaliation. The conversation lulled and Clive felt the pull of Randal's gaze upon him. His fork stopped halfway to his mouth and his eyes were drawn forcefully towards the point of contact. A luminous film covered the slate-grey pupils and Randal's voice spoke to him telepathically.

Marcus and his saintly grandfather are both dead men walking.

Clive's heart sank. It was far too late for any lectures. Randal would be meticulous in executing his revenge. And there was absolutely nothing he could do about it. Nothing at all.

★★★

Alison was waiting in ardent anticipation for Randal. She was expecting him at any minute, as they had made whispered plans over dinner. She lay naked in the dark in her large four-poster bed wondering if she was being somewhat too forward for their second weekend together. Then she giggled out loud at her doubts. What did it matter? They had made love before and it was so complete. It was only natural for her to be ready for him.

He knocked twice and her toes curled round with a tingling sensation as her heart began to thud. He opened the door and glided slowly over to the bed. He was naked underneath his robe. He discarded it and she pulled back the sheets so he could join her and her whole body began to tremble as she felt his irresistible nudity against her own.

"Hi," he said huskily against her lips, "I've waited all day for this."

His mouth came down on hers, as he pulled her to him and she felt his manhood pulsating with desire. Their breathing became heavier until they were breathless with abandon. His hands were everywhere all at once and she arched against him showing him the extent of her longing.

He used his long, slim fingers to drive her mad, exploring the most secret parts of her body. As if that was not enough, he followed the same intimate trail with his mouth but as much as she rejoiced in his foreplay, she needed his entry more.

He was fighting to keep a tight rein on his lust. She welcomed his thrusting penetration and moaned out loud with the invasion. With every rapid push he rasped out her name, whispering a stream of lustful endearments against her mouth which excited her beyond endurance. She opened her legs even wider to accommodate him. They reached their highest peaks together and she squealed with the ecstasy of it all.

They lay side by side in the aftermath of their intense lovemaking. No words, as yet, had been uttered since. Randal just kept stroking the length of her body; up and down, as if he could not get enough of her form and nearness.

After a while she spoke.

"I'm on the pill because I want you all the time," she murmured.

"Do you now?"

"Tell me you love me," she rasped into his ear.

"More than anything or anyone," he whispered, caressing her face.

"I need you, Randal," she moaned.

"Then prove it; prove it again," he urged in a thick voice, grinding his hips against her own, causing an instant response as she pushed up against him urgently.

Alison lost count of the times they made love. Randal's expert technique drove her insane, and in return, she inflamed his senses with her untamed reactions, over and over again.

★★★

Late into the night Marcus was sitting on a chair at the side of his grandfather's bed, discussing the day's events. Leslie wanted to play down his apprehension but at the same time he could not lie about his feelings.

"The boy is possessed," he confided, "there's a lot of darkness within and around him."

"Possessed? You mean a satanic spirit of some kind?" asked Marcus frowning deeply.

"I don't know exactly but I do know this, that whatever it is, it's not a holy emanation. We're dealing with something quite evil. Something… how shall I put it? Something totally and utterly oblivious to sacred matters. I've got to say that, as a priest, I can't stand by and do nothing in its wake," said Leslie with grim determination.

"Have you come across anything like it before?" half-whispered Marcus, as if he was afraid of Randal picking up on their conversation.

"No. No, never," admitted Leslie.

Marcus was starting to feel very sorry for ever bringing the matter to his grandfather's attention. It was all beginning to get out of hand. He rubbed both of his arms as if the heat had gone out of his body.

"Do you mind if I smoke?" he asked, reaching into his trouser pocket for his cigarettes and lighter.

The Reverend shook his head and Marcus lit up the first one he pulled out of the pack with trembling fingers. He dragged hard on its filter tip for reassurance. He blew out a vapour stream and watched it drift across the room, curl around the opulent chandelier on the ceiling, and then disappear into thin air.

"It's in his eyes, isn't it? Those X-ray eyes of his that burn into your brain. It's as if you have no secrets. None at all," said Marcus staring into space.

Leslie reached out to him and touched his hand. Marcus looked at him earnestly and returned the gesture.

"Gramps, can't we just let this drop? Now that I know that I'm right about him and that you can feel it too, well I guess we could just keep out of his way," he said feebly.

"It's not that easy," claimed Leslie. "It knows, you see. It knows why you asked him here. Don't you understand, Marcus? Let's not forget that he's the one in torment and ultimately needs our help. He probably doesn't even realise the extent of his possession. Once an evil spirit lives inside a person, he's not responsible for his thoughts or deeds. We must exorcise this demonic presence out of his soul."

"Must we?" asked Marcus quavering with fear. "I'd rather turn my back on the whole issue. He's dangerous, Gramps."

"He's not dangerous; his possession is. I know what I'm talking about. We must help him, Marcus, because if we don't, every single person he touches in his lifetime will be damned."

★★★

Lady Pennington was having a sleepless night. Every time she closed her eyes, Randal's vivid image flashed into her mind with alarming clarity. She tossed and turned with an unfamiliar restlessness, her head throbbing with unwanted infidelity. *This is ridiculous*, she kept telling herself as Randal's features swamped her senses once more. She could not understand how she could think such lustful things about a youth, exactly the same age as Marcus. Her youngest son, Thomas, was at boarding school. Anyway, she was in love with her husband of twenty-five years, so why was she hankering after forbidden fruit? These were alien feelings and went against the very grain of her ethical background. She had always been intensely loyal to Miles and had never before entertained such a dangerous longing.

She got up hurriedly out of bed and put on a peach silk dressing gown over her matching nightdress, with the intention of finding a good book to read until she felt sleepy. She descended the secondary stair into the library lobby, past the walls hung with prize whips and crops, which were the trophies of Miles's great-uncle, Charles Pennington. She switched on the lights, pushing her long dark hair behind her ears, as she browsed through the endless rows of reading matter, trying to find something that would occupy her mind. After about ten minutes, she concluded that it was a pointless task.

Fiona decided that she needed a stiff drink and made her way downstairs to the boudoir, which she regarded as her own. She often received close friends here and also conducted her correspondence in the privacy of its walls. Although she was not a habitual drinker, she kept a small selection of spirits in a compartment to the left of her desk and now found herself pouring a large brandy, swirling its rich amber liquid around the glass, before practically knocking it back in one. Sitting down on her chair, she helped herself to another measure. She sipped distractedly at the warm, soothing mixture, continuously tapping her long, manicured fingernails on the tabletop, as she stared into space.

Two sharp knocks on the door brought her quickly out of her trance, as she jumped nervously with the interruption. She wrapped her dressing gown tightly around her as she made her way over to the caller. She caught sight of the time and saw it was only four o'clock and wondered who was up and about so early in the morning. It was probably Adams, checking to see if everything was all right and she was not quite sure what she was going to say to him by way of an explanation.

Fully dressed and framed in the doorway, leaning slightly sideways in a lazy, arrogant stance, Randal greeted her with a sexy smile, as she peered up at his face.

"Sorry to bother you, Lady Pennington, but I saw the light on and wondered who was up at such an untimely hour. Now I know that it's you, well, I can relax," he said in a suggestive tone.

Her heart leaped out of her chest and returned just in time to alleviate her complete breathlessness. A few moments elapsed before she realised that she still had the brandy glass in her hand and she had said nothing in response to his presence. The shock of coming face to face with her dream lover had rendered her speechless.

Randal's unique eyes glittered and moved appreciatively over her flushed features, then trailed indolently over her shapely body, making her incredibly aware of his appraisal. She felt an unacceptable heat between her legs and it left her shamefaced and dumbfounded.

Randal continued the conversation when he saw her reaction to his presence.

"I was too hot to sleep, so I took a walk around the Hall. I hope you don't mind. Anyway, I was just about to go back to bed when I saw a light underneath this door, so I thought I'd better check on the occupant, to see if everything was OK," he explained, looking into her brandy glass.

"Oh," was all she could reply.

"Well is it?" smiled Randal, amused by the effect he was having upon her.

"Is what?" she asked, thinking how silly she sounded.

"Is… everything… OK?" he repeated slowly, as if he was addressing a confused child.

"Oh, yes, everything's just fine. There's nothing to worry about. I'm the same as you. You know… hot. It's a very warm night and I… um… can't sleep," she said stumbling over her words and feeling embarrassed by her feeble explanation.

"May I join you?" he asked in an old-fashioned manner.

"Well I am rather tired," she answered demurely.

Randal put on his little-boy-lost mask that always proved instantly effective with the fairer sex. It never failed to tug at the female heartstrings. Fiona melted at the sight and his boyishness brought a smile to her beautifully shaped mouth.

"Well, perhaps for a little while then," she agreed in response to his artificially crestfallen expression.

"Thank you, ma'am," smiled Randal as he saluted her, clicking his heels together in a mocking military gesture.

Her laugh was appealing as she let him into the room. He decided that he would not stay too long because he had left Alison in bed fast asleep, exhausted by their furious lovemaking through the night. He, on the other hand, was wide awake, because all the physical activity had imbued him with an even greater sexual energy, which was not entirely spent.

"Would you like something to drink?" offered Fiona unassertively.

"I'll have the same as you," he replied, pointing towards the brandy bottle but not taking his eyes off her face.

She filled his glass and her hand trembled as he took it off her, deliberately trailing his fingers through her own.

"Cheers," he said with an intense expression on his handsome face.

"Cheers," she just about responded.

She felt a white heat shoot through her body at the look of consuming physical attraction in his compelling eyes.

Randal felt the captivating urge to slide his hand inside her silky gown and explore the skin underneath. The events of the past twenty-four hours were swirling around in his head and contributing towards his present state. Alison's total submission; the beauty of his surroundings; Clive's jealousy; Marcus's and the old priest's combined deception; his thoughts of vengeance; they all blended together and excited him immeasurably.

It was one of those licentious nights and he felt very immoral and in a position of extended profligacy. All this debauchery was in his fiery, sparking eyes and the sight of Fiona's slim but curvy form only intensified his inflamed passion.

His desire communicated itself to her and she could hardly breathe. Her sense of loyalty and morality screamed out its objection to his impertinence but she felt a traitorous combustion roar through her bloodstream, pumping the hot red fluid around her veins and arteries, like volcanic lava preparing to erupt out of the impassioned heat from within.

She watched him put down both their glasses and then move towards her in slow motion, his eyes scorching into her own. Her long eyelashes feathered her cheeks, as she lowered her burning gaze.

"Look at me," he ordered hoarsely.

She wanted so badly to object to his command but her treacherous body refused to obey her guilty conscience. She did as he wished and his mouth came down on hers with such force, that his teeth pierced her bottom lip and drew blood. The pain became an unbearable pleasure as the contact altered into a warm, passionate kiss, which sent shockwaves of desire through her whole body. All righteous thoughts were shoved aside as he ravaged her senses and made her forget who and where she was.

Randal lifted her up, moving away the pen and papers on the desktop in one fierce swoop, to make space for her to sit down. Having done so, he pushed open her limbs with his knee and dragged her nearer, pulling her legs around his waist. He opened the front of her dressing gown and felt the shape of her breasts through the silk of her nightdress, rubbing his thumbs against their hard tips. His excitement was mounting and she felt his hardness through the thin material, as he pushed and pressed against her urgently. His arousal was so strong; it seemed hard to believe that he had made love repeatedly to Alison beforehand.

Fiona was the first much-older woman he had ever wanted to possess. She was exquisite and her small scented frame seemed to melt into his own. Against all her religious upbringing, she succumbed to his lust and helped him to remove her nightwear so that she was completely naked for his invasion.

She unbuttoned his shirt and pressed her bare breasts wantonly against his hard chest, getting immense pleasure from the sound of his heavy breathing. She undid his belt and slid it out of its loops, letting it fall to the floor. Her small deft fingers unzipped his jeans and reached inside to release his throbbing manhood from its restrictive area and she felt its hot thickness pulsating in her hand. Some kind of madness had taken over her mind causing her to behave in a manner that she would thoroughly condemn in others but she could not fight it because she had reached the point of no return.

Her hand reached out to stroke him and he felt an unbearable excitement in his loins. He played with her lovely breasts then bent his head to kiss them both, his hot tongue flicking from one to the other across each swollen tip. Fiona squirmed with the sensation but she wanted more and told him so by positioning herself just above his pulsating member. She moved down on to him slowly, feeling him slide effortlessly inside her body, until she was full of his passion. She knotted her legs around his middle as he pulled her shapely buttocks towards him, to achieve an even tighter and deeper grip.

He began to thrust inside her, showing her no mercy or tenderness but this is what she wanted from him anyway. She threw back her head in complete abandon as he kneaded her breasts, leaving bruises wherever he squeezed and pressed. Her hands kept clasping and unclasping on his broad shoulders and her long nails dug into his young flesh, as he drove deeper into her body, with a desperate urgency born out of sheer lust.

"Faster!" she cried in a strangled voice.

"Is this fast enough for you, milady?" he breathed raggedly against her lips.

Randal could feel the unmistakable stirrings of his much-needed orgasm and had no intentions of delaying its release. He stepped up his rhythm, doubling up on each thrust to let Fiona know he was about to climax. She had already reached her high spot several times, but the sensation stayed with her, as he kept bringing her to repeated peaks. He cried out as he gushed deeply inside her and she gloried in the look of unbearable ecstasy on his frenzied face.

For some time afterwards, he was still plunging inside her body with a subconscious reflex action, but after a while the movement subsided and then stopped.

When he pulled out of her, she felt bereft. She was still seated on the top of her desk and began to shiver, her skin goose-bumping with the coolness of the room and his physical departure from within her. Tears were beginning to slide down her cheeks now that the spell had been broken and the harsh reality of her flagrant infidelity hit home. Randal picked up on her mortification and held her head in his hands, stroking her hair in a gesture of comfort, as he kissed the tip of her nose.

"Don't be ashamed. It happened because we both wanted it to and it was so, so good. I promise you this: nobody will ever know," he said gently, as he helped her put on her nightdress, lifting up her chin so that he could look into her eyes.

Her mouth trembled with gratitude. She did not trust herself to speak and remained seated as she watched him conceal his glistening manhood back into his jeans. He zipped up his fly and walked away, holding his belt. He looked round at her.

"If ever you need me, Lady Pennington, just call," he smiled suggestively in the doorway then made his way back to Alison.

Fiona's head was beginning to thud and she felt sick with shame for committing the most unpardonable sin.

How could she possibly face her husband and family now that Randal had so quickly stamped his lascivious brand of sexuality on her soul?

★★★

Sunday morning saw everyone sitting at the breakfast table except the Lady of the Hall and her father. Fiona had managed to pull herself together in a fashion and return to her chamber. Once there, she just lay on her side in the bed, feeling the warmth of her husband's body next to her own, as she wept quietly for a while, eventually falling into an exhausted sleep. When Miles awoke, he presumed she was overtired and left her alone to dream.

After Fiona's father had eaten, he took advantage of the warm spring morning, strolling slowly through the surrounding woodland, before going to church. Ironically, most of the family did not attend regular services, except Fiona, but he did not want to disturb her. Everything seemed upside-down but there were only twenty-four hours remaining of Randal's visit and Leslie had taken certain steps to make sure that he did not act suspiciously, or fearfully, in his company.

Marcus was shattered. He had been wrestling with his thoughts for most of the night and felt very ill at ease with Randal's dark presence in his family home. He knew from the start that he was playing with a hellish fire but he thought he could control it. That is what he told himself until he saw his grandfather's ashen face when he introduced him to their demonic guest. His plans to get closer to Clive had taken a back seat. He still felt that Clive knew most of the answers to his questions about Randal's shadowy side but he wondered if he was worth the danger it most certainly involved.

In contrast, Alison had not felt so relaxed and happy with herself in a long time. The weekend was turning into an ideal vacation. She chewed her toast and scrambled egg, wishing she could stay longer in the stately setting and in her lover's bed. Randal had snatched a few hours' sleep with Alison before creeping back into his own room to shower and dress for breakfast. He was inwardly amused.

Talk about musical beds. I better wash away the sweat and perfume on my skin from all the recent activity. I'm not worried about facing the Lady of the Hall over her muesli because she won't be there but that's not to say I've pulled the plug on that particular dalliance. She's definitely worth a repeat performance!

The others had taken their places and Miles began to chat to Clive over breakfast. He wanted to know more about his son's close friend and Clive responded well, finding his natural gregarious manner once more after being swamped by Randal's suffocating charisma the night before.

Miles thought it a great pity that Fiona could not see this side of Clive and felt she had jumped to the wrong conclusion about his personality. Randal let Clive take centre stage. It suited him that Miles was otherwise occupied and not asking too many questions.

Although Randal loved Alison more than life itself, he still felt incredibly physically drawn towards Lady Pennington and wanted to repeat his wanton performance with her before he left Clarendon and returned to Oxford. There would be plenty of time later to also charm her husband, and ensure he was not in any way aware of Randal's lustful intentions towards his wife.

Besides, he had to secure himself a return visit or two before he finally decided the fate of her father and son, when he would put a definite and inclement finish to their amateur witch-hunting.

For the rest of the morning they split into twos, each duo spending their time doing different things. Marcus took Clive on a walking tour of the Estate observing the wildlife and then they drove around the farmland, which was home to many more species of birds. He parked the car in a quiet place so that they could just sit and talk but it was hard-going because both of them were very much aware of Randal's effect upon the household and unsure of whether to approach the subject. They sat in silence watching a tumbling display of lapwings, and because the crops were only half-grown, they saw a few rabbits scampering around the fields.

"Smoke?" asked Marcus, offering Clive a cigarette, who nodded back in silent confirmation.

Marcus lit them both and then gave one to Clive. They both sat in their seats, inhaling deeply and blowing out tobacco fumes in silent contemplation. They spoke at exactly the same time, then apologised to each other for the overlap.

"You first," said the pair of them together and laughed at the additional cross-timing.

They smiled at each other and Marcus was suddenly aroused by Clive's nearness. *That bloody Randal Forbes*, he cursed inside. Here he was, in close proximity to Clive, wanting so badly to reach out and tell him how he felt and it had all gone so terribly wrong. It was a bitter-sweet situation and Marcus was sure that Clive was hiding vital information, so how could he have a close relationship with someone who was holding out on him? He had to take the bull by the horns and voice his doubts and fears because he knew he would not have another chance quite like this. It was the perfect time and place, away from prying eyes.

"About Randal," he said, coming straight to the point and he saw Clive brace himself.

"What about him?"

"I know he's, shall we say, drawn to the occult. I believe that he's taken on board some kind of dark vitality that lives inside him. I don't know exactly what it is, but I think… I think that you do. I've got to tell you, Clive, that my grandfather is very tuned into it and very disturbed by it; not only for other people in its path but also for Randal himself."

Clive always knew that one day, someone, somewhere, somehow, would put him in the daunting position he was in right now. He did not expect it quite so soon. He had thought that when Randal made his mark on the world with his genius, curiosity and analysis of his 'gift' would be rife. Clive respected Marcus highly and knew that he would not be palmed off with some feeble explanation but at the same time he was very angry with him for his deception over Randal's invitation.

"Why couldn't you speak to me about your suspicions instead of playing detective with your family?" was all Clive said in response.

"I had to find him out, Clive, and my grandfather knows about these matters. I've suspected for quite some time that Randal has hidden dark powers. I've tried talking to you about his stranglehold over you. It's not normal. You always fob me off. You won't hear a bloody thing against him. You put up with monumental shit from him! Why? What are you hiding? Are you afraid of him? Afraid he might hurt you? What's the real reason?" urged Marcus.

"The real reason? Oh, just believe me, Marcus, you wouldn't want to know," winced Clive.

"Try me," he persisted, putting his hand on Clive's knee.

Clive's hand shook slightly as he took another drag of his cigarette. He had never been so close to divulging Randal's secret. He felt a sense of overwhelming concern and protectiveness from Marcus. He knew it was genuine and for the first time in his life, he was considering betraying his lover's trust. This weekend's performance was only the latest saga in a long line of emotional upheavals, all in the name of Randal Forbes, and he was weary of the burden.

"Try me," repeated Marcus, sensing that Clive was weakening and on the verge of a sensational revelation.

Suddenly Clive's conscience felt heavy with guilt.

What the hell am I thinking of? Randal's confided in me, and me alone. I know the score. He couldn't have made it clearer to me. I'm the only lesser mortal on this planet who knows about 'the gift'. I'm letting my human frailty colour my common sense. Randal's my life. I've been chosen to protect him and I can't, I simply can't allow the truth to be unearthed.

Marcus watched intently as Clive opened the car door and got out. He walked to the front and sat on its bonnet, still smoking and seeing nothing in particular. Marcus let him sit on his own for a while and then joined him. He stroked his face in a loving gesture of solidarity.

"I care about you, Clive," he murmured.

"I care about you too but…"

"But?"

"But…"

"You care about Randal more," deduced Marcus sourly.

"Yes, I do, heaven help me. He's wonderful but hateful. He's kind but very cruel. He gives but takes. He nurtures but corrupts. He's dynamic but demonic. I adore him. I always have and I always will and when you love somebody like that, you take on board everything there is. The good and the bad. In Randal's case the good and the evil. Dear God, Marcus, you've no idea how much evil," he concluded wearily.

He looked at Marcus for sympathy and understanding; for silent empathy. And it was then that Marcus knew for sure. Clive, in the simplest way possible, had told him that his grandfather's theory was wrong. Wrong in the sense of a satanic spirit living within. Wrong because it was Randal who was demonic. Whatever dark powers he possessed were his very own. There was no ill-lit, bodiless living being manipulating his deeds. Marcus shuddered involuntarily as the enormity of Clive's revelation sank in and his thoughts became riotous.

Hell, and high water! We're all fucked! Randal Forbes is his own Antichrist!

***

Randal and Alison did not want to look further afield and were quite happy to stay within Clarendon's grounds. There was still much to see and they were both interested in the history of the Hall.

"Would it be all right, Lord Pennington, to go exploring around the Estate?" Randal asked Miles over breakfast, smirking to himself about his wife's wild submission.

"Of course; you must," he replied enthusiastically.

Alison linked her arm through Randal's as they wandered around for a while. They found themselves in the basement, curious to see how the servants used to live below stairs. They entered a large old room, which for the past fifty years had been used as a coal cellar but was originally the servants' hall. Randal soaked up the atmosphere of long ago.

"This must be the wine cellar and now we're entering the housekeeper's room and finally the gun and rod rooms," explained Randal with an innate sense of knowledge.

"Just look at this kitchen, Randal, it's so ancient but fascinating," enthused Alison, as she stopped to run her hand over the charcoal stewing stove, trying to imagine the cook of the house at work in past times.

"Let's go see the courtyard and the old potting shed. Apparently, it's still equipped with the traditional garden tools from the early 1900s," added Randal.

They found their way back to the grounds and decided to have another slow walk around the beautiful gardens. The weather was mild and they meandered in and out of the scented displays, arms around each other in a natural closeness.

Upstairs, in the confines of her bedroom, Fiona stirred and awoke. She yawned widely and stretched her aching muscles, feeling lethargic. Her head felt heavy and she tasted the remnants of sour brandy in her mouth. Then she remembered and her insides turned over, making her feel sick with remorse. She wanted to stay in her bed, covering herself over and never leaving its sanctuary. Perhaps she could say that she felt unwell and that way she would not have to face him; that would be the best thing to do while Randal was still a guest in the Hall.

Randal. She whispered his name in her mind. Dear Lord, even now she was still full of him. Maybe if she prayed very hard, like she did as a child, her guilt would diminish. She desperately needed to wash away the smell of immoral sex on her skin. The room felt stuffy, so she moved the curtain to one side in order to open the large front window. She caught sight of two figures, walking arm in arm around the grounds. When she saw it was Randal, a sudden rush of heat shot through her, as if she had been physically assaulted from a distance.

His arm tightened around Alison as he stroked her face and hair lovingly and Fiona was shocked by her insane jealousy over the fact. Then suddenly, without warning, he looked up towards her and as Alison nestled comfortably in the curve of his broad shoulder, he blew Fiona two elaborate kisses, meant for her eyes only. Consequently, she was even more alarmed by the thrilling intensity that all was not lost and that Randal still harboured the need to possess her again.

I want him. All over me. Inside me. And I know he feels the same. God forgive me!

5

Randal spent a large part of summer 1977 exploring Cumbria with Clive. After the hectic social and academic whirl of his first year at Beaumont, he felt the need to escape into the rural splendour of the Lakeland Fells. He was confident of the results of his recent exams; the all-important tests as to whether he would be accepted for a second year of studies. He made absolutely sure that Clive would once again be with him by giving him a telepathic helping hand with his syllabus; entering his brain, and boosting Clive's own abundant knowledge of his chosen subject.

He had returned three times to Clarendon Hall since his first visit; once with Clive and twice on his own. Alison had also been invited but was too busy with musical projects and touring but she had written to the Penningtons, thanking them for thinking of her. The invitations had been signed by Lord and Lady Pennington but had really come from Fiona. Marcus observed with absolute dread how much his mother was 'taken' with Randal, but even he could never have guessed the extent and depth of her all-consuming fascination. It was bad enough having the devil under his ancestral roof at his parent's request.

Fiona was utterly obsessed. She would observe Randal talking to her husband, Miles, taking the opportunity to study him very closely. The further she tried to justify her infidelity, the guiltier she felt about the object of her fixation. She had given Randal several expensive gifts, wanting to pamper him in more ways than one. He had turned her into a wayward siren and she lived in fear of her family's revulsion if they should ever discover her scandalous secret.

Randal thought about Fiona a great deal.

I've got a lot of respect for Lady Pennington. She's not a natural adulteress and I've corrupted her. She excites me and the need to possess her has not diminished. She's definitely on a sensual pedestal and I've developed quite a passion for her aristocratic submission. Very strange. I want her as much as Alison. Other women are just for casual sex. I tire of them all so easily. But not the Lady of the manor.

After his talk with Clive, Marcus had instructed his grandfather to close the book.

"Gramps, forget the exorcism. Randal has his own built-in demonism. Clive told me and I'm seriously scared, so let's drop the whole idea."

"Utter nonsense, Marcus. The boy is possessed and needs holy assistance."

Marcus was at a loss to know what to do next. One thing was certain. He could not leave his family to the mercy of satanic wrath and he owed it to them to stick by his grandfather's side.

Randal, as always, was fully aware of the thoughts and would-be deeds of the people around him. He had already mapped out the fate of Marcus Pennington and Reverend Leslie Stainthorpe. He pulled a face that matched his escalating vengeful thoughts. *If only they would take a hike and stop trying to expose me, then they could all live happily ever after in their own inferior utopia. But some people never learn and ultimately have to pay the price for the unearthing of things best left alone. So, my sweet Fiona, I still intend to forge ahead with your father's and son's removals from this earthly plane. But I'll comfort you selflessly after the deadly event.*

★★★

When *Telesthesia* was staged in the College Hall in the seventh week of Trinity Term, Randal's name was on most people's lips and Beaumont boasted a dramatic society, quite unrivalled for activity in Oxford. The play was well received by the college judges and scooped top prize for production and originality. Edward, Margaret and Patricia had travelled down to see Randal's latest offering and were hugely impressed by his creative genius and acting ability. Later on, they were introduced to the cast at the after-show party.

Margaret and Patricia were both struck by Robbie Sterling's likeness to Dean. Margaret especially had watched him on stage, admiring his performance and thinking how amazingly similar his features were to her young nephew's. Afterwards they all socialised.

"Congratulations on a superb performance, young man," enthused Margaret to Robbie, "are you thinking of going into dramatics professionally?"

"Oh no, not at all, it's just a relaxing and rewarding hobby. Randal's script was the obvious attraction. I'm studying medicine and setting my sights on becoming a consultant physician. I want to make my mother proud when she sees the name of Dr John Sterling on the medical board," he elaborated with a wide smile.

"John Sterling? I thought your name was Robbie?" she questioned through tight lips, the mention of Dottie's deceased married lover, and Dean's real father, stirring up best-forgotten memories.

"No, Robbie's my middle name. I've the same first name as my late father, but they called me Robbie to avoid confusion and it stuck."

"Late father?" whispered Margaret, praying that her suspicion was totally unfounded and it was all a horrible coincidence.

"Yes… he died when I was very small. It was all so long ago. It was tragic you see. He was… he was… murdered. I told Randal and he's been very sympathetic and has helped me enormously. I'm really grateful. He gave me a leading role in this wonderful production and I'll never forget his kindness and friendship. He's a very special person; a genius but a philanthropist too. Clive as well. They're both such good friends and have helped me overcome my demons."

"I see."

"Anyway, enough of me. May I get you another drink, Mrs Forbes?"

"You can get me one, if you like. I'm Randal's sister," intercepted Patricia, weaving her way towards him through the crowd.

She looked stunning in a figure-hugging, aquamarine, crushed velvet dress. Her fair hair had been bobbed and the feathery fringe rested just above her deep blue eyes; her natural exuberance and zest for life glowed on her lovely face. Robbie's eyes kept travelling along the length of her body then trailed slowly around her features, very much aware of her beauty.

Margaret needed to get Randal alone and ask him point-blank whether she had just been conversing with Dean's lost family. She was desperate to know.

Margaret did not care for the way Robbie was assessing her daughter. Patricia's response was even more worrying, as she preened and posed with dramatic gestures, showing that she was equally attracted to him.

"Excuse me, I'm just going to have a word with Randal," she said and they nodded.

He was holding court with an entourage of students who were clustering around him in worshipping droves. Margaret made her way through them to tap him on his shoulder.

"I need a word, Randal. Somewhere very private please," she urged with a stern expression.

Randal picked up on her concern and frowned. He left his admirers to join her and they vacated the room. Margaret cleared her throat before she spoke.

"I've just found out that Robbie's real name is John Sterling and I don't have to tell you the significance, do I?" she probed.

Margaret could have sworn that her son's eyes were slightly aglow. They were in a dark corridor and the expression in them was very daunting. They glistened with a sinister strangeness she had never seen before.

"Are you listening to me? Robbie's the image of Dean! He has the same name as Dean's deceased father and your Aunty Dottie told me that John had children at the time of her affair with him! Randal, tell me the truth. Is he Dean's half-brother? I need to know what's going on!" she concluded sharply, pulling at his arm. She was irritated by his lack of response to her questioning and slightly nervous of the weird way he was gazing into the space behind her.

Her vexation brought him out of his hellish trance and he looked down directly into her line of vision. Once again, she caught the alien gleam in his eyes and the air turned chilly around them. She put it down to the ancient stone floors and walls of the college and the coolness of the evening.

She did not realise how hard he was struggling to contain his wrath because he did not want his mother to know the full extent of his hatred; how he loathed and despised Robbie and his late father. He had to play it all low-key.

Cool it. If I'm going to have a major hand in Robbie's demise I can't afford to be seen as a prime suspect. I've cultivated an open friendship with him both personally and professionally, to show people that he's part of my inner circle. Don't blow it now.

"I hoped you wouldn't find out, Mum. I didn't want to tell you because after our graduations, we'll both go our separate ways. There's no need to inform Dean because what he's never had, he'll never miss. Who told you?"

"Robbie did! He wants to be Dr John Sterling! For God's sake, Randal, what are you thinking of? His father broke your Aunty Dottie's heart into little pieces! It's not Robbie's fault, I know, but did you have to get so close to him?" she admonished.

Randal still felt confident of his plans until the door opened and his inebriated sister came tumbling in, linking her arm through Robbie's and laughing at his every word.

"I wondered where you two had got to. Daddy's looking for you both," slurred Patricia and then giggled with the effect of too much wine.

"Really," acknowledged Margaret in a cold voice but her daughter was far too giddy to hear the disapproving tone in her mother's reply.

Robbie could see that Margaret was far from pleased. He thought her a little rigid because this was, after all, a celebration of Randal's literary triumph. It was only natural that her daughter should want to toast her brother's success.

"Patricia's told me she's just had a year's gruelling study for her exams. She's only merry-making, Mrs Forbes. I'll look after her. She's in safe hands," assured Robbie courteously.

"Robbie and I are going walkies. Do you want to come?" she hiccupped, putting her head on his shoulder.

"The fresh air will do her good. It's too stuffy back there. You can't hear yourself think with all the noise," smiled Robbie.

Randal's face was half in shadow and the dim light in the corridor gave him a sinister appearance. His heart was beating very fast, rather like it had as a child, when he was most displeased, or on the verge of revenge. His reaction disturbed him because for the first time in years, he felt out of control.

The sight of Patricia, in such close proximity to John Sterling's son, made him want to vomit.

The mongrel wants to screw my sister! Why didn't I see this coming? I didn't expect her to come to Oxford at all. She looks amazing but I was far too preoccupied with the staging of my play to forecast any problems.

Mum said she was still away but she obviously changed her plans and voila! Here she is! And look who the fuck she's with now!

He was furious with himself for not even suspecting, let alone forecasting, something like this could happen and even more livid with Robbie for befriending his sibling and plying her with wine.

Son-of-a-bitch and offspring-of-a-toerag! This was not meant to happen on my big day! Always someone spoiling the perfection!

His eyes were starting to glow and he needed to use every ounce of his willpower to stop his spiralling rage. He had to make this right.

"It's OK, Mum," he heard himself lie. "Robbie's right. She needs fresh air. Let her go with him."

Patricia blew him a noisy kiss in appreciation and then tottered unsteadily away from her mother's disgust and her brother's repugnance.

Blast it to hell and Hades! Now my destructive plans for Robbie Sterling will have to be the number-one priority and put into immediate effect. Marcus and the old priest will be dealt with at a later date. I'll have to put my removal cap on. Right now!

"Mum, don't freak out. Robbie's no threat. At first, I was really shocked by the discovery but as I got to know him, I realised that none of his late father's sickening traits run through his veins and he can't be held responsible for his mistakes," appeased Randal outwardly, but inwardly he was seething.

"I don't like the way she's becoming rapidly attached to him, Randal; flirting and acting like a besotted lush," scorned Margaret.

"Mum, it's just a crush and the booze. She's letting her hair down. There's an exciting atmosphere here and it's affecting her mood. That's all it is," pacified Randal feeling far from reassured because he felt they had really clicked.

"I hope you're right; I truly do," sighed Margaret as they returned to the other room to join everyone.

Not long after Patricia's visit, Randal received a letter from her, asking for more information about Robbie and his background. She had disguised her eagerness in a comical style of writing but Randal could read between the lines. He scowled at her interest. He perused the end of the letter and it put him in a bad mood for the rest of the day as he read her request.

Is it possible that I could stay with you at Beaumont? You could tell Robbie I'm coming down to Oxford again in the next week or so maybe? Please Rand, I think he's really dishy. Don't tell him I said that! Hope to see you soon (and him!) Love you, Patricia xxx

On top of her letter, Robbie had also been asking questions about Patricia, pumping Randal on more than one occasion.

"If I were you, Robbie, I'd look elsewhere. She's involved with a boy back in Cheshire and it's pretty heavy," he lied.

"Shame. I really like her… more than like her. We may have become related in the end, Randal," he half-joked.

That remark was far too close to home and Randal wasted no time telephoning his sister that same evening.

"Hi blondie. How you doing?"

"Oh, hi Rand. Did you get my letter?" she asked eagerly.

"Yeah I did. Look sis, about Robbie. I know you're keen but I have to tell you that he's pretty involved with a medical student in his year. They've been seeing each other and she's head over heels about him and vice-versa. I'm really surprised he didn't mention it," he lied.

"Oh, I see. He never told me that," she replied in a flat voice.

"Don't worry; you're gorgeous. There's more than one guy for you sweetheart. Look around and take your time."

Randal was pleased with his deceit. He had hit upon a simple solution to keep them apart for now. It had given him more time to play with, in making sure that their separation would be a permanent feature.

★★★

It was while he was rambling with Clive in the Lake District that he decided to get in touch with Robbie and ask him to join them for the last week of their stay. He phoned him from one of the youth hostels in Carrock Fell.

"Hey there, Doctor Who! Put away that stethoscope and get yourself down here. You'll love it; so many hills and valleys to explore and country pubs! It'll definitely appeal to your adventurous side. Anyway, we both miss you," flattered Randal and Robbie fell for it hook, line and sinker.

When he met up with them, he found that Randal had hired bikes and had already planned their route for the day. After greeting each other enthusiastically, they made their way along the Lakeland tracks, laughing like overgrown school boys as they rode up steep hills, panting furiously with the effort and then standing on the pedals as they accelerated hazardously down gradients.

"It's a bloody good job you're a medical man in case there's a mishap!" yelled Clive as his tyres slid all over the place into saturated soil and silted runnels. Liquid sheets of diluted mud spurted from his wheel rims but he stayed firmly in his saddle, his bike mimicking the movements of a bucking horse.

"Hold tight!" shouted Randal as they surfed down another treacherous slope, their bottoms lifting in unison off their seats on a gravitational wave.

It was very hard-going and sometimes they had to get off their bikes to push them up the steeper hills. The descents were stimulating and they clung on hard to their handlebars and brakes, their palms itching and fingers becoming rigid with the juddering downhill movements.

"Tomorrow we'll explore on foot," said Randal to the groaning twosome behind him, as they welcomed a level surface of road.

"Tomorrow I'll be dead," rasped Robbie, through dry lips, feeling the exhausting effects of the last few hours on his system and discovering muscles and tendons he had only read about in his medical books.

Randal smirked and cogitated.

Oh, you'll be dead all right, sunshine. But not tomorrow. In the next few days.

As they turned around a bend in the surface road, they found the beginnings of civilisation. They cycled past the church and post office and then a cake shop, with the most delicious home-made baking prominently displayed in the front window. They reached a central point within the village itself and although the traffic was rather minimal, they still got off their bikes and wheeled them along the pavement, looking for a pub to quench their thirst.

"I could murder a pint," groaned Robbie, licking his lips in anticipation.

Randal smirked inwardly again and identified with the verb more than the drink.

The weather had turned humid and a storm was brewing. The sweat trickled down their bodies. An ice-cold lager would not go amiss with a shady corner to rest their aching limbs.

They found a public house close by and secured their bikes in the car park at the rear. They could smell the ale before they reached the bar, as the front door had been wedged open to let in what little air there was on such a sultry day.

"The first round's on me. Go and play some pool. Oh, and Clive, put The Beatles, Dylan and Bowie on the jukebox," ordered Randal.

Clive saluted then punched in the numbers for each song, as Robbie set up the table for a game of pool. On the surface it all looked extremely amicable to the village regulars, who weighed up the young strangers in a curious, but inoffensive, fashion.

Randal brought the drinks over and sat back lazily in a comfortable chair, seemingly relaxed and content, while Clive and Robbie vied against each other, chalking up their cues and points, in between large sips of beer. Clive gave a whoop of delight at potting yet another ball from a tricky angle.

"Yabadabadoo!" he gloated, Fred Flintstone-style.

"Beginners' luck; jammy sod," scoffed Robbie and looked over at Randal, raising his eyes to the ceiling in playful camaraderie.

Randal smiled back at him, disguising his utter contempt. His mind was ticking over like a preset time bomb, intent on inflicting maximum damage.

I'll let you have your five minutes of fun. Patricia rang me before I left for Cumbria. She told me that she'd received a letter from you, followed by a phone call or two. Slimeball. You went against my advice and decided to pursue her after all. Even my mythical boyfriend tale didn't put you off and even though I told her you had a steady girlfriend, that didn't cool her ardour either because you coaxed her into your two-faced Sterling net. You're finished!

He could not take the chance of his sister becoming emotionally or intimately involved with John Sterling's son. Patricia was headstrong and Robbie was smitten. It would only be a matter of time before they became a couple. It was a fact that the more a person tried to oppose the coming together of two people intent on a relationship, the opposite would happen. It would unite them rather than pull them apart.

He had planned his itinerary the night before he telephoned Robbie to join him and Clive in Cumbria. He could not waste a minute longer in plotting his cessation of life. It would be done quickly and cleanly. The setting was perfect. A sheet of bolt lightning flashed across the inky sky and the thunderclouds rolled boldly in the distance. The oncoming storm inspired Randal's dark side.

Oh yes. There have been many, many mishaps reported over the years in the Lakeland Fells.

I can't wait to put the show on the road. Even my bike is excited. I must try and be patient because this has to be executed well. No mistakes.

Therefore, Dr John Robbie Sterling, it won't look at all abnormal or suspicious if you were to have an unfortunate 'accident' in the breadth of these majestic peaks and deep valleys.

For the next few days they ditched their bikes and rambled. They met up with a variety of people along their way, including a lively party of students from Scandinavia who were celebrating their postgraduate status. They spent a whole day in their company and Robbie became particularly friendly with a Swedish girl, Ingrid, who spoke English well, and was also studying medicine back in Stockholm. They hit it off instantly and discussed all the current strides of progress in their field.

Randal observed how quickly they had become attached and it angered him, adding even more fuel to his grievances. The sight of their two heads together in theoretical collusion, only reinforced his desire to rid Patricia of her infatuation. Games were not allowed. Robbie was not going to practise tricks with his sister's emotions and be permitted to breathe.

A wind had sprung up by the time they moved on. Robbie swapped addresses with his Swedish admirer and they parted warmly. Randal seethed.

They needed a place to stay for the night and had been told of a nearby inn, which did bed and breakfast at a reasonable cost. The three of them headed there, following the twisting and winding track, sometimes muddy through thorn and gorse, but with the compensation of the glorious mountainous horizon. Randal proposed that they make a temporary detour in order to view the sights from the high fells, so that he could take some extra photographs for his album.

They climbed upward as the force of the wind increased. Clive stumbled over some loose rock and Robbie grabbed his arm to stop him falling over.

"I think we've gone far enough, Randal. You can get some brilliant pics from this spot. There's no need to go any further," advised Robbie.

"You can both stay here and wait for me. I'm heading for the top of the crag. There's a stunning aspect from that particular angle," replied Randal, progressing upward as he spoke.

"Yeah, but just watch it. It's slippery territory up there," advised Clive with a note of caution in his voice.

"No sweat; just hang on for me. I won't be too long," he replied and they observed in admiration as Randal deftly tackled the tricky ascent, until he found a sheltered spot out of their sight and the persistent wind.

He sat on a couch of stone and dry heather and took a few snapshots of the expansive landscape all around. He stood up and photographed the wild, craggy beauty of his surroundings, admiring the way the sun kissed the lakes, thinking that the steel-grey of the mountain range was not dissimilar to the colour of his eyes.

Then he called upon 'the gift'.

It had been a long time since he had done so and it felt almost orgasmic in its emergence. His eyes glowed with a hellish radiance and blazed with unmistakable luminosity, in a stream of bedevilled light.

He fused with the elements and felt the irrepressible rapture of his interstellar power and force.

Robbie had been talking about Randal's literary genius and telling Clive he was looking forward to future creations. Clive crossed his fingers that Randal had changed his mind with regard to Robbie's fate. It all seemed cordial but that did not mean a thing. Clive began to extol Randal's endless virtues, in the usual obsessive manner, when Robbie suddenly felt very odd. Clive's voice sounded remote as if it was coming from a great distance.

The wind whistled around them and whipped up a dense cloud of dust. The powdery particles blew into Clive's eyes and mouth, stopping him in mid-sentence.

"Damn it!" he exclaimed, as he spat out the grimy dirt and sheltered his pricking eyes with his hands. He turned his back to the blustery wind and brought out a handkerchief from his trouser pocket, wiping furiously under the rims of his invaded eyelids.

Robbie felt as if an intruder was ransacking his brain. He could hear a voice inside his mind issuing commands. His medical knowledge kept battling against the mental chaos, seeking a self-diagnosis. The voice became louder and clearer as he struggled to maintain his sanity.

I want you to go to the edge of the cliff. Don't fight me, just do as I say.

Robbie's strong, practical nature was at odds with the instruction he had been given but his will felt assailed and he was now under the control of his dark invader. He moved forward and turned off the track towards the perimeter of the sheer drop into the valley below. A raven flew overhead, riding high on the wind, wings streamlined into a steeply angled dive, as it skimmed the crag. He felt the softness of mossy cushions underneath his feet and walked further towards the lichen-covered rocks. When he reached the given point, he stood still, leaning against the wind as the voice spoke to him again.

Now listen closely, medical meathead. I'm your destiny. Your waste-of-space father defiled my Aunty Dottie when you were a child and left his filthy pollution inside her. He made her pregnant and then offered her money to abort his seed but she refused and I aborted your papa instead. I was his assassin. Now, one of his more wholesome sperm created your half-brother. His name is Dean. He'll be twice the man you are. Or should I say, you were?

Even in his hypnotic state Robbie felt himself start to tremble. This was a nightmare from which he would surely awaken at any moment. He was in some kind of deep, dark dream because events like this did not happen in reality. He looked downward and saw the tangle of heather fronds and ledges of hard, dry rock below.

The mighty summits of the surrounding mountains hogged the limelight momentarily and then Randal's voice seemed to bounce off them all, travelling faster than the speed of sound into his subconscious.

You'll never get the chance to defile my sister. I would have killed you anyway if you had sullied her with your Sterling charms. I'm just doing it sooner than later. Don't you think I'm considerate?

Robbie kept forcing himself to wake up. He tried to block out Randal's terrifying words but they just kept coming at him from some untapped dimension.

Randal kept playing with Robbie's thought processes, torturing him with dark messages. It was his every intention to prolong his agony, making the last moments of his life a deliberate infliction of pain and terror. Randal's cruelty knew no bounds and 'the gift' was now in full flow as he raised his arms and incandescent eyes upwards. He fused with the wind-driven clouds and the sun broke through, spoiling the effect of his dark silhouette against the sky. Wavy patches of sunlight crept over him and he drank in all the textures and movements. The landscape played an impassioned tune to his spirit and he encroached even further inside Robbie's mind.

Did you enjoy playing opposite me in my play? It will be the first of many for me but not for you. You performed well. You would have made a good actor but you wanted to be a doctor, didn't you? Saving undeserved lives would have suited you. Your daddy was an undeserved life. Enough said. Now please do as I say and move closer to the edge. Are you ready?

Robbie was screaming inside but nothing was coming out of his mouth. How could he hear Randal so clearly and not see him? Where the hell was Clive? Couldn't he detect what was happening? Didn't he hear the same evil words? But, how could he? It was all a hideous dream. None of it was real. He could control this phantom reverie himself, if he just concentrated more to banish its delusion. Randal threw back his head and laughed harshly at Robbie's defiance and the unearthly sound shattered his floundering resolve.

You're such a pathetic clown! This isn't a dream! If you hear my voice then it's my voice! If you feel fear, you feel real fear! So, when I tell you to jump, you'll jump! Now, prepare to die!

Robbie shuffled his feet into their last position at the edge of the cliff. There was nothing left to do but obey. To offer resistance of any form was just to delay the inevitable. A buzzard swooped overhead and two plumes of smoke could be seen moving northwards from a steam train in the distance.

Clive managed to get most of the grit out of his eyes. He did not see Robbie right away because he was looking in the wrong direction. When he did, he called out his name, but it was too late. He shrank back in horror as Robbie threw himself off the perpendicular face of rock. Clive raced towards the edge and shook violently as he caught sight of the crumpled, twisted body far below. He screamed out for Randal but there was no sign of him.

He scrambled wildly upward, in exactly the same direction that Randal had taken beforehand, and tripped over twice, gashing his flesh on a jagged boulder, but he felt no pain. He clambered further and then spotted Randal sitting in a sheltered location, out of the wind. He threw himself upon him with an inaudible explanation of what he had just seen but there was no response.

He knelt in front of him and put his arms around his neck. He looked up at him and came face to face with the smouldering embers of 'the gift'. Clive's mouth dropped open at the remaining glistening aura of Randal's unmistakable demonic stance, boldly defiant in the face of his crime.

"Why? Dear God, why?" sobbed Clive unashamedly.

And Randal's stony silence spoke volumes, and told him all he needed to know.

★★★

The grim details of Robbie's death were described in the newspapers as 'a tragic misadventure' and although Randal wanted his and Clive's identities kept out of the report, this did not deter the journalists from naming them. As there were no other witnesses, the police questioned them both closely about their movements, before Robbie's fatal slip and thereafter.

"One minute he was OK and the next he just stumbled. I'm devastated and I blame myself. If I hadn't asked him to join us, then he'd still be alive," admitted Randal passionately. "That blustery wind didn't help. It was hard to even stand up."

He was always at his most plausible after committing the perfect telepathic crime. He performed well for his interrogators with a faultless act of believable contrition, injecting just the right amount of emotion into his statement and excusing Clive's lack of cooperation as delayed shock.

"I assure you, officer, we're both deeply disturbed by our friend's crushing death."

"And you, Mr Hargreaves? I know you're traumatised but can you remember anything?"

Clive shook his head and a solitary tear rolled out the corner of his eye.

They came home to face a barrage of questions from their families and friends. Clive felt drained of all emotion. Robbie's untimely and violent end had shaken him badly. His death was dire enough but the real facts behind it were even worse. No words had been spoken between him and Randal. It had all been swept away under a silent, conspiratorial carpet where it lay dormant, far too repugnant to mention. Deep down Clive had always known that Randal had a cruel, ulterior motive for befriending Robbie. Clive's love for Randal was presently undergoing its greatest test.

How could I have fallen for the devil's disciple and still want to be at his side? But what would I say to the police? That Randal murdered Robbie with his mind and willed him to jump off the cliff? That would go down well at the Old Bailey. I'll have to carry the villainous truth around with me for the rest of my life. But where will it all stop? He's only just on the threshold of success and that will bring more enemies. My head's going to burst. I've got to get away from him and think it all over. I've got to work it all out.

Randal knew that Clive was going through a self-imposed crisis. It was only to be expected in the extreme circumstances. He would give him time to come out of his soul-searching dilemma and heavy conscience.

Their exam results had been successful and they had both been accepted for a second year at Beaumont in six weeks' time. Randal was completely confident that Clive would be at his beck and call by then; a little jaded perhaps, but definitely still as besotted.

They were good together. It had been written that way. He would continue to teach him how to control his human emotions and put aside his personal feelings with regard to any traumatic telepathic reprisal.

Eventually, Randal knew that Clive would accept that 'the gift' was more important than one mortal entity, no matter how young or old that life may be.

★★★

In his Manchester hospital, Dr Patrick Shaw was having lunch. He saw the article on Robbie's death in the paper. He had only read a few lines when Randal's name leaped out at him from the printed page, putting paid to any more enjoyment of his meal. By the time he had finished reading the report he was one thousand per cent convinced that Randal was the sole cause of John Robbie Sterling's premature burial.

He had contacted his friend, Chief Inspector Leonard Galloway, who phoned him back with the latest report.

"I've pulled a few strings with the Cumbrian constabulary to obtain a copy of Randal's statement. It appears he was genuinely devastated by it all. There's not the slightest contradiction in his evidence. If anything, Patrick, it's a bit too believable with perfect credibility. I've read your compiled catalogue of past candidates on Randal's psychic hit list and among them was the name of the deceased's late father, so I'm well aware of the paternal connection with regard to Dean Thornton and John Sterling."

"You know something, for some time now I've been thinking of shelving my probing into Randal's strange powers for fear of putting my own family in danger. Regardless of his affection for my wife, Victoria, I feel he's indescribably evil, with a total disregard for the sanctity of life. He could remove anyone in his way, or on his case, without a moment's hesitation or contrition. Who can really say what lengths he would go to, in order to protect his dark rights?" shuddered Patrick.

"Do you want to shelve the investigation?" asked Leonard.

"My fellow medics would think me unhinged if I were to tell them this. As fantastic as it all sounds, I'm sure that Randal's linked into some dangerous, dark force that he calls upon in the name of his own weird and twisted sense of poetic justice. What's more, I believe there could be others like him dotted around the world, forming some kind of sacrilegious network of damnation, each unknown to the other, but equally powerful in their own neck of the woods. The repercussions of that theory would be far too mind-blowing to contemplate at this stage."

"So, what are you saying? Are you warning me off, or just going over your fears?"

"I've kept all this away from Victoria. She's besotted with his genius and what she sees as his amazing psychic ability that will save the world. She would be livid if she knew of my probing and your involvement. Do you believe me Leonard? Do you feel the same way about his paranormal crimes? Do you believe that he's telepathic but using his powers inappropriately, to say the least?"

"I'm not totally convinced but I admit there's something very strange going on, so I would still like to pursue it all, and keep a beady eye on his movements."

"That's your prerogative, Leonard, but I need to ask you whether you'll take over from me in the role of prime investigator? I have to think of my wife and children. I feel terribly guilty in passing it all across to you, but I must, I simply must shelve this obsessive probing."

Leonard assured him that he was willing to step into his shoes but Patrick was afraid for him; afraid that Leonard would end up as a prisoner of his own fate and that Randal would be the eternal keeper of his wretched soul.

6

Patricia sat in front of her dressing table looking forlornly into the mirror. She had recently been accepted at Sheffield University and was due to start her first term in a week's time. She would be reading French and should be feeling excited at the thought of a new chapter in her life but instead her heart felt heavy with sadness, for a love affair that she would never have. Even though she had only been in Robbie's company the one time, he had been inside her head ever since and she had felt sure that they would have got together, had he lived.

When Randal returned home, she needed to ask him countless questions about the tragic event.

"How could Robbie fall over a cliff so easily? Where were you and Clive? Couldn't you have saved him? It's upset me so much. It's too cruel. His family have been robbed. He died much too soon," she affirmed with a sob.

"He slipped. It was very windy. Sis, I know for a fact that he wanted to take you out. He spoke very highly of you and even asked me if it would be all right to date you. He was prepared to finish with his long-term girlfriend for you. I really rated him," he lied through clenched teeth. He kissed her cheek tenderly and wiped away her tears as she wept quietly in the circle of his strong arms, while he cursed the memory of his latest victim.

At the request of Robbie's two sisters, Randal and Clive did not attend his funeral. They preferred a small private service and thought that if Randal had not contacted their brother to join him, he would still be alive, although they could never have guessed at how near the mark they were with that conclusion. Their mother, who had been living with a sporadic depressive illness ever since their father was murdered, relapsed completely when she heard of Robbie's fatal 'accident'. Her head could not cope with such a damaging, devastating blow. She switched off her mind into its own level of awareness, which would allow her to perceive, see and think on a safe plateau of consciousness.

Margaret had not said anything to Dottie about meeting Robbie in Oxford. When his death was reported in the paper, with his full name and photograph, Dottie had telephoned her instantly and asked her outright if he was related to Dean's late father. Margaret's silence provided her with the answer she was dreading.

"God, Maggie! Why didn't you tell me about him?"

"And say what? That Dean's half-brother was Randal's new friend and that he fancied Patricia and the feeling was mutual?"

"Patricia! What's she got to do with it all?" exclaimed Dottie.

"They met and hit it off when we went down to see Randal's play. Robbie had a starring role in the production and they got together afterwards. Randal said it was just a whim, but Patricia's been depressed ever since the accident and I think her feelings ran a lot deeper than any of us realised."

Dottie felt physically sick at the mere thought of her niece being emotionally involved with John Sterling's eldest son and was struck dumb for a moment or two.

"Hello? Dottie are you still there?"

"Yes, yes I'm here," she answered, feeling the waves of nausea slowly subside, as she struggled to come to terms with her shock discovery.

"Hell, I wanted so much to spare you all this. That's why I said nothing. I was mostly worried about a possible involvement with Patricia but Randal reassured me that it would pass," sighed Margaret.

"Well it doesn't matter now, does it?" whispered Dottie.

"It's tragic. Randal's handling it well considering he and Clive were there when it happened. Clive? Well, he's not so good. His mother phoned me last night and said he's in bits."

Dottie felt a wave of depression wash over her, reviving best-forgotten memories of a tainted past.

"Did he… did Robbie have other siblings apart from his sisters? John never really elaborated on that," asked Dottie unexpectedly.

"Just the two sisters I believe."

Dean's lost family, they both thought.

"Dottie, we'll get together this weekend and, in the meantime, you must phone me if you need to talk in between. Don't hesitate. Promise?"

"Promise."

Dottie put down the receiver and returned to the newspaper article. The photograph of Robbie dominated the page and looked at her with Dean's eyes. It was so extremely ironic, and deeply sad, that John Sterling's only surviving son was the one he had wanted to abort. Dottie had never wished any badness on his wife and children. They were blameless and equal victims of his dirty game. There were no real winners in a situation such as this.

Her life was so full and complete now. Her marriage to Neil Gibson and her legal career were both flourishing. Dean was a happy and healthy twelve-year-old, secure in the love that his mother and stepfather provided him with. Dottie remembered how lost and alone she had felt when John had deserted her as she carried his baby. That hurt and vulnerable girl had vanished, and in her place stood a confident young woman, wife and mother. As she gazed again at Robbie's handsome image the telephone rang. It was her medical centre with the outcome of a blood test that her doctor had requested.

She thanked his secretary at the other end of the line. The result was positive, just as she had thought. This could not have happened at a more poignant moment and an emotional lump started to form in her throat as the news sank in. Her fingers began to shake as she dialled the number for Neil's office.

"Darling," she spoke softly as he answered. "It's me and I've got the most wonderful news. I'm pregnant."

★★★

Dean's reaction to the news that he was going to be a brother was one of delight. He instantly became very protective of Dottie, suggesting that she handled a much lighter workload and that her welfare came first and not that of her clients. He was pleased for her and his stepfather, Neil, but his main priority was his mother.

"After all, you're going on thirty-six, Mum. You've got to watch it at your age," he advised one night when she decided to clean out a kitchen cupboard to make more storage space.

"And you're twelve going on thirty-something! Good grief, Dean, I'm not made of porcelain and I won't break if I drop!" she snapped, feeling like his patient, under constant medical surveillance.

His features crumpled at her sharp words and she immediately felt guilty. She stopped wiping down the shelf and walked over to him at the table, where he was doing his homework, in between keeping a beady eye on her activities.

"Sorry, Dean, I didn't mean to be cross with you but you must understand that I know my own body and if I think I'm doing too much, I'll stop and take a rest. You mustn't treat me like an invalid. I mean let's face it, I've had a baby before and he didn't turn out so bad. Did he? Huh?" she concluded, tugging at both of his ears like she used to do when he was little.

Dean smiled, pulling Dottie's ears in return and then running both his hands through her newly cut short hair, messing up the style.

"You look like Johnny Rotten," he giggled as his bright blue eyes lit up with amusement.

Dottie felt a wave of pure love for him and hoped that the baby she was carrying would have the same sweet, thoughtful nature.

"What's going on here then?" asked Neil as he walked into the room and saw his wife's wild hair. "You look like Ken Dodd."

Dean fell forward in hysterics in his chair as Dottie made her teeth appear goofy, then grabbed hold of the feather duster, in homage to the Liverpool comedian.

Neil watched them clowning around and thought what a lucky man he was to have such a loving wife and stepson. He was elated that Dottie was having their baby and thought of Dean as his very own. He was going to suggest that he should adopt him legally and the birth of their newborn would complete the family picture.

All Neil ever thought about was Dottie and Dean and the things he could do to make them safe and happy.

Randal had intermittently tuned in to Neil's head. He had to make sure that his special Aunty Dottie and beloved Dean were being looked after in the way they deserved. Hurting or abandoning them was not allowed.

Consequently, Randal thoroughly approved of Neil's objectives, giving them both something in common. It was just that Randal's method of achieving the same result was rather more spectacular in its execution.

★★★

Clive picked up the telephone to speak to Randal, but halfway through dialling, he replaced the handset. He repeated the same action three times, but in the end, he gave up and switched on the radio instead. The music made no difference to his state of mind, even though it was one of his favourite songs. In a week's time he would be resuming a new term at Beaumont College with him and they had not spoken to each other for a month, ever since their fraught journey home from Cumbria. He had felt a roller coaster of emotional chaos since then.

At first, he cried a lot because he felt guilt-ridden over Robbie's death but then after the tears, there came great anger towards Randal, but mostly at himself for keeping quiet when questioned about the tragedy. There followed a short period when he fluctuated between resentment and despair. Clive's thoughts had tormented him.

I wish I could tell Mum and Dad. This would all be so much easier if I wasn't a satanic stooge. I've had countless nightmares about Robbie. He's always begging me to protect him and save him from Randal's wrath. I keep reliving the horror of his fatal leap to eternity. Over and over again.

Clive's main problem lay in the fact that Robbie had been a friend. More recently he had come to realise that if he had not known him personally, and Randal had done away with a faceless name, he would not have taken it to heart in quite the same way. All things considered, he concluded that had the victim been a stranger, he would have forgiven Randal. Eventually his deliberations became more rational.

I'm a hypocrite! What right have I got to condemn him at all? It's only because I knew Robbie. I'm being judgemental and yet I'd have overlooked this removal if the wretch was unknown to me. Randal wouldn't kill a person for nothing. Would he? Just for the sake of a cheap thrill? Just to demonstrate 'the gift'? It was obviously necessary even though it's very hard to understand from a humane viewpoint but there again, Randal isn't purely human!

Paul and Rosemary Hargreaves were very concerned about Clive's state of mind and had been in touch with Randal's parents a number of times over the fact.

"I wonder if Randal could help? I think they should get together and talk the whole thing over," Rosemary suggested to Margaret.

"Randal's coping. Don't take this the wrong way, Rosemary, but he thinks that Clive should have counselling. He feels that his presence would only remind him of the tragedy and it would be better for him to consult a complete outsider."

"You know, I think Randal's right. I'll suggest it to Clive," she replied thoughtfully.

When the call had finished, she went upstairs to Clive's bedroom and found him looking out of the window, staring into space.

"Clive darling, I was wondering if you should speak to a professional therapist about your depression? They would help you to cope and get back to your sunny self."

Even in his depressed state Clive laughed inwardly. A shrink was the last person who would believe him. If he did not want to be committed on a permanent basis, the best thing to do would be to keep the whole truth under wraps and learn to live with it all, without psychiatric care.

★★★

Marcus was sat with his grandfather in the picturesque grounds of Clarendon Hall, like a one-man grand jury who had unanimously found Randal guilty of Robbie Sterling's murder in the first degree.

"I know it was him! There's not one person who can tell me otherwise," groaned Marcus, as he lit up his second cigarette in the space of ten minutes.

"You're smoking too much," the Reverend scolded, "and anyway, I still feel that the boy is possessed and not in control of his actions."

"Bullshit! The evil son-of-a-bitch is in control all right! That's the bloody trouble," replied Marcus caustically.

"Shush now! Keep your voice down and at the same time mind your language! There's little point in taking that attitude, Marcus. It won't get us anywhere," scolded Leslie.

"I'm sorry, Gramps, but can't you see that Randal's his own problem? There's no demon in the driving seat because he's the controller, not the controlled. We can't save him but we can bloody well protect ourselves by keeping well away from him. I feel hugely responsible for his visits to Clarendon, especially the fact that my mother has developed an obsessive madness for his company and swears that the sun shines out of his satanic backside," he grimaced.

"Marcus!" chided the Reverend but he was instantly interrupted.

"Just listen to me!" pleaded Marcus, clasping his grandfather's hands in his own. "I want, no, I *need* you, to stop this right now! Forget any holy redemption or exorcism that you have in mind for him! Please just drop it! I don't want to argue with you any more and I'm seriously scared by what I feel! The guy's dangerous! He's evil and that's all there is to it! Let it go, Gramps! Let it go!"

Leslie looked at the terrified expression on his grandson's face and began to reconsider his priorities. He could see that Marcus was holding himself solely responsible for Randal's presence in their lives.

Perhaps he should stand back and let this take its own course without any interaction. His religious conscience cried out that Randal's soul was spiritually violated but he would abandon all interplay, in favour of Marcus's welfare.

Like his grandson, he was also puzzled and perturbed as to why Fiona had formed such an obvious penchant for

Randal's visits. When he had declared his uneasiness to her about Randal's dark nature, she had thrown her head back and laughed harshly in his face. Her reaction startled him because it was so out of character.

"Really, Daddy! You and Marcus are so out of line! Randal possessed? He's absolutely charming. Where on earth did you get that hideous idea from? Are you both bored with your lives? Ridiculous!" she snapped.

Leslie would have to somehow convince Fiona to discourage any more contact with him because if Marcus was correct in his theory, even the strongest form of exorcism would be powerless against such an inborn and unholy abomination, who masqueraded under the name of Randal Forbes.

★★★

Randal had rented some rooms for himself and Clive just outside the town centre in Oxford. He had secured them in advance because as second-year students, they would not be living in the college and had to find their own accommodation. Their new home was on the first floor of a large Victorian house, which had been converted into flats, and was only a ten-minute walk from Beaumont. Even though Clive had not been in touch with him, Randal was quietly confident that it would not be too long before they reunited.

Sure enough, Clive had taken the bull by the horns and had called round on an impulse to see Randal, one week before they resumed university life. His heart thumped as he rang the doorbell, not really knowing what sort of reception he was going to get after his long absence. It was Margaret who greeted him enthusiastically and kissed him on both cheeks.

"Oh Clive! I'm so delighted to see you! Come into the lounge. How are you?"

"Better than I was."

"That's wonderful. Randal's studying in his bedroom. I'll go and tell him you're here," Margaret said quietly, absolutely relieved to see her son's closest friend return to the fold. "He'll be thrilled. I won't be a minute."

Clive sat down on the large settee, breathing in the familiarity of the tasteful surroundings. His heart kept skipping beats and his palms began to sweat in anticipation of their reunion.

"He's coming down. Would you like a cup of tea? I can't tell you how pleased I am to see you, Clive. Let's not talk about the incident. It's gone and now you and Randal have to get on with your lives," she advised, as she came back into the room.

"I think I will have some tea and perhaps some of your unbeatable apple pie if there's any going spare?" he smiled, glad that she knew why he had stayed away and had thankfully come out of his depression. Almost.

"Hello you."

They both looked up together as Randal's tall frame sailed through the door. He was dressed from head to toe in black and Clive gave him a score of eleven out of ten for maximum sexual impact. He seemed to glide across the floor as he walked towards them, fully aware that Clive had gone weak at the knees and was glad to be already sitting down.

He drank in Randal's suffocating nearness and every single negative thought that he had been wrestling with over the last few months was blitzed into thin air at the glorious, seductive sight towering before him.

"Good to see you," said Randal warmly, along with his special smile.

The expression in his steel-grey eyes was so vastly different from that awful monstrous afterglow, when Clive had found him sat in smug disregard, following Robbie's induced, fatal leap. Clive's heart lurched as he remembered but then it altered into its usual drumbeat rhythm at the sight of Randal's seductiveness. A chain of erotic thoughts invaded his head, making it hard for him to act normally.

Margaret disappeared into the kitchen. She knew they would want to catch up and for the first time in weeks they were completely alone. Randal moved nearer to Clive but he jumped up off the couch knowing full well that his touch would reduce him to a quivering wreck and he did not want to fall so readily back into his arms, without making a stand. He walked towards the fireplace and stood with his back to Randal, resting one foot upon the hearth.

"I can't just go back to how it was at the snap of your fingers," said Clive in a flat voice, not knowing if he was punishing himself more.

"OK, let's talk about it then," replied Randal, willing to go along at his friend's pace if that was what he wanted.

But Randal really knew that Clive was trembling inside for physical contact.

"It took me ages to come to terms with Robbie's death and what you did. I… I still love you but I had doubts over the last month or so, when I convinced myself that I actually hated you. But I've come through all that analysis now," added Clive with more conviction than he actually felt.

"Good. I'm glad."

"Good? You're glad? Is that all you have to say!" snapped Clive, his body heat rising with the lack of emotion in Randal's response as he turned around.

"What do you want me to say? You know the score. I did what I had to do. I'm sorry if you got burned by it all but that's not my fault. It had to be done," he replied unfeelingly.

"You monster! You murderer!" retorted Clive, his cheeks reddening.

"OK. I'm a monster, or a murderer. Take your pick, but here's the thing. I've missed you. Badly! I need you by my side and in my bed," affirmed Randal, narrowing his gaze with sexual intimation and the look threw Clive completely off balance.

Randal moved closer and Clive fought extremely hard to maintain his tight-lipped expression. But it was useless.

"Don't fight me. What's the point? Hmm?"

Randal touched the side of Clive's face and an electric shock went through his whole body. In a robotic fashion he found himself falling into Randal's embrace and he knew that no spell had been woven to make him so responsive. It was just a natural continuity of the deep love that he felt and their recent separation had only enhanced the urgent need for an immediate reconciliation of body and mind.

They had to hide the fire burning in their eyes and cover their erections with their hands, as Margaret returned with tea and cake. "Enjoy! Now do help yourself, Clive, to a huge slice of apple pie," she smiled widely, then left them once more, taking great joy from their reunion.

But as soon as the door closed it was Randal who helped himself to a huge slice of Clive's endless adoration.

★★★

Chief Inspector Leonard Galloway was sat at his desk reading the details that Patrick had compiled on Randal's movements. He bit on the end of his pen then scratched his head as he studied all the information, including a meticulous hit list of alleged victims that had all been, one way or another, connected with Randal over the years. Alongside each name, Patrick had written an explanation, as to why, how and when they had allegedly been affected.

Jeremy Newton (aged 9) Tarnside Primary School; a bully who was traumatised into a state of paralysis by Randal, leaving him mentally disturbed for life.

December 1964

Alice Hardman (headmistress of Tarnside Primary School). She suspected that Randal was evil and to blame for Newton's infirmity. She met up with Randal's parents at their house, to inform them of her opinion. Randal found out and hypnotised her into leaving the assembly hall in school. He then ordered her to strip off her clothes and jump naked into the swimming pool, where she drowned in an induced state of paralysis.

December 1964. Official verdict: suicide.

Dottie Gibson (nee Thornton), Randal's aunt. He found out she was pregnant by John Sterling, a married man with children, who apparently wanted her to abort his baby. Randal orchestrated his revenge by tuning into Sterling's head, possibly through a photographic image and somehow caused his death by exploding glass.

April 1965. Official verdict: murder (unsolved).

Dean Thornton, born October 1965 (Randal's maternal cousin).

Patricia Forbes, Randal's sister, told my wife, Victoria, about the family holiday in Killarney, Ireland. From what I could make out, Patricia developed a childish crush on an American boy called Blake. He left earlier than planned because he was hallucinating and affecting the other guests. It's likely that Randal caused it for his own amusement because he did not care for Blake.

Summer 1967

Randal met Alison Whitaker (classical pianist and girlfriend) in January 1968.

Edward Forbes's 40th birthday party; the coming together of the whole family and my first encounter with Randal. Alison was requested to play a piano piece but it began unusually badly for a gifted musician. In retrospect, I remember that Randal was very annoyed with her for skipping her music lessons with his mother, as she was dating an art

student instead. I saw his eyes kindle. He could have entered her head causing her to strike the wrong notes out of spite.
  October 1968

William and Ashley Forbes and wives were due to fly out to France for a holiday together. The night before, I was called out to treat Randal who had felt ill and dizzy. I think that he had a premonition that their plane was going to crash so he engineered a form of epilepsy on himself resulting in hospitalisation. He even had me fooled. The family cancelled their holiday and sure enough, their flight crash-landed, killing all on board. Randal was still in hospital 'recovering' but he did not care about the other fatalities. He probably thought nobody would believe his premonition anyway, so it was the only way to save his family by injuring himself. Magnanimous but still vile.
  Summer 1973…

Leonard paused to make a fresh cup of coffee. He sat back down and flicked over the page to the next list of names and events that Patrick had put together.

… Simon Holmes, fellow student at Redwood. On the receiving end of Randal's wrath for bullying Clive Hargreaves. Ended up in the same condition as Jeremy Newton.
  June 1974

Heather Fielding, Randal's maternal cousin. Randal, together with family, and Clive, all visited her in Southport. Her two Labradors attacked him, maybe sensing an evil aura. Then they uncharacteristically turned on Heather. She was hospitalised with extensive injuries to her face and body. I feel that Randal stopped the attack against himself telepathically and then caused the dogs to ravage Heather instead.
  July 1975

Dean Thornton, Randal's maternal cousin, discovered the sordid truth about his birth father, through fellow pupil, Nick Haynes, in a callous way. Randal took revenge by eliminating the whole of the Haynes family. He could have entered Raymond Haynes's head telepathically (Nick's father) and incited him to kill Delia Haynes (mother) with a carving knife.

October 1975. Official verdict: manslaughter, diminished responsibility.

Nick Haynes and his two sisters, Lorraine and Jill, chose to live with their maternal grandparents after their mother's death and father's arrest. They went for a walk through the local park and bumped into Randal and his cousin, Dean, who stopped to speak to them all. They go their separate ways but I believe that Randal, out of sight, telepathically entered the heads of the three children, and hypnotised them into drowning in the lake. I think he planned the whole tragic and repulsive event.

January 1976. Official verdicts: accidental death.

Randal receives an unconditional offer from Beaumont College, Oxford, and begins his studies there with his friend Clive Hargreaves. I'm sure he knows about Randal's dark side and protects him. I also feel there is a same-sex relationship.

October 1976

Randal's book 'Poetic Justice' is published. For the most part it points towards his involvement with all the aforementioned crimes but is cleverly disguised.

February 1977

Randal meets John Robbie Sterling (Robbie) at his drama society. He picks him to play a leading part in his new play. He discovers that Robbie is, in fact, his cousin Dean's half-brother, which would enrage him. Randal's sister, Patricia, meets Robbie after the staging of the play and partners him for the night. Randal's mother, Margaret, isn't happy about the liaison either. Randal spends the summer holidays in Cumbria with Clive and invites Robbie to join them. On their last day, Randal wills him to jump off a cliff face. I should imagine it was done in much the same way as he hypnotised Alice Hardman to jump into the school swimming pool. Randal gave a statement to the police because Clive was speechless with shock.

Summer 1977. Official verdict: misadventure resulting in accidental death.

Leonard frowned deeply. If the validity of Patrick's theory was correct, then they were sitting on some kind of psychic bombshell and Randal was now a prime suspect as a serial killer; albeit a telepathic assassin, with no conscience or regret.

★★★

Two weeks into the 1977 Michaelmas term, Randal began mentally ticking off the days on his calendar to Monday, 31st October. He had planned his own black magic ritual to coincide with the time of year that his notorious self-penned poem described in such great detail: Halloween.

His nerve endings tingled and his heartbeat quickened with the thought of his next elaborate secret scheme. It was to be a glorious example of excruciating diabolism and he could hardly wait to carry it out into effect. As with all his other sitting targets, he would feel a complete justification in their annihilation. Fortuitously, he would be seeing and screwing Lady Pennington on the coming Saturday, at her invitation, and that suited his itinerary perfectly.

Marcus had unwillingly cooled his attention towards Clive because he did not want to come into contact with Randal and it appeared to have worked because he kept out of their way. Clive was enormously relieved that Marcus was keeping his distance.

Randal was driving more frequently. On the morning he was due to go to Clarendon, the weather turned unusually mild for the time of year. Randal showered thoroughly, pampering his toned body with scented gel and washing his coppery red hair with an expensive shampoo, which were both gifts from Fiona.

Her generosity pleases me. I'm very much in the mood for her services. Oops! I don't want this huge erection now. I want the Lady of the Hall. Better save it for the real thing and not some erotic forethought.

He left Clive fast asleep in bed, leaving him a note to say that he felt like a drive and not to worry if he was not back in time for lunch.

He won't surface until early afternoon anyway; not after that pub crawl, we went on last night. Most of my circle will be very much the worse for wear today I expect. Except me of course. It'll take more than half a bottle of Jack Daniels to dampen my ardour. I'm immune.

As he drove along the country roads, he switched on the car radio and whistled the tune of a latest song. Fiona had told him that she had the Hall to herself, apart from Adams and his wife. Lord Pennington was out of town for the day and would not return until late evening. Her father, the Reverend, was busy with church matters and she would not be seeing him until tomorrow. Marcus had gone down to London with some fellow students and her younger son, Thomas, was back at boarding school.

The coast will be clear for me and milady. Oops! Here comes that whopping hard-on again. Down boy! Think of something else; something completely different to take your mind off her honeypot.

He took the next bend in the road with reckless speed and forced himself to think of anything other than his sexual desire. He was using this visit for a dual purpose and his mind dwelt upon its real significance. In the boot of his car was a black canvas holdall and its contents were of the utmost importance to his latest plan of action. He smiled cruelly at the reason for its usage. It was simple really. All he had to do was hide it somewhere in Clarendon Hall's grounds.

On Halloween, Marcus would be the one to find it in order to carry out his bidding.

★★★

On the last day of October, Marcus had just finished an afternoon tutorial, when he felt the strangest compulsion to contact his grandfather. The desire was so strong, that he found the nearest public telephone box to ring him and he was relieved that he was at home.

"Hi, Gramps, it's me. Are you in tonight? I'd like to drive over and see you."

"Of course you can. There's nothing wrong is there?" enquired Leslie, thinking it most unusual for his eldest grandson to make a visit on a Monday evening.

"No, nothing's up. I just feel like a chat," replied Marcus, not really knowing why he did.

"Well that's fine then. I'll look forward to seeing you; shall we say at eight?"

"Ideal. See you soon then."

All the way back to his flat, Marcus could not understand why he felt it was important to see his grandfather. He was very fond of him but that did not explain the sudden craving for his company. Tonight, he had been invited to a Halloween party with some friends and knowing the host, it would be an outrageous gathering of intellectual rabble. He had been thinking about Clive a lot lately, so a wild orgy would have been the perfect distraction.

Later that day, he decided to have something to eat before he drove to Banbury. He made his way to a popular pub for students in the town centre. As he entered the smoke-filled room, he bumped into a few familiar faces.

"I can't believe you're not coming to the party, Marcus! It's going to be so cool," protested a fellow student, pushing his shoulder playfully.

"Yeah… well… I need to see my grandfather and then I also have to be up early for an important tutorial," smiled Marcus and his companions jeered.

"What a king-size drag you've become. Is your aristocracy making you inhibited? I thought your sort were decadent. My mistake," mocked a student from his course.

Marcus laughed as he ordered his meal and spent some time with them all chatting about various college news.

"Oh well, I'm sorry but I've got to scoot now," said Marcus looking at his watch.

"Off to grandfather in his respectable rectory?"

"Get lost! Anyway, all of you reprobates, have a good night," he said sarcastically.

"Oh, we will, but will you?" another would-be reveller mocked.

Marcus put two fingers up at him as he left the table and laughed as his parting gesture was returned.

I still don't understand why I have to see Gramps tonight. Something's pulling me there. Oh well, Banbury here I come.

Marcus crossed over the road to where he had parked his car, feeling for the keys in his coat pocket. He saw that it was sandwiched in between two other badly stationed vehicles and swore to himself inwardly. He had a problem pulling out of the confined space but after some clever manoeuvring, managed to position himself in the right direction.

As he left Oxford, he took the Banbury road.

There were two ways to his grandfather's rectory. One of them would actually take him practically past the doorstep of Clarendon Hall; the other was more direct and of a much shorter distance. He had no intentions of seeing his parents so he opted for the quicker route, yet for some peculiar reason he found himself taking the road to his ancestral home instead. He frowned deeply and tutted.

How the hell did I miss the turn-off? How on earth did that happen?

Suddenly his head felt very heavy and his vision began to blur, so he pulled into a lay-by out of harm's way. The feeling began to intensify to such a degree that he almost fainted from the swirling sensations. Then, just as unexpectedly, all the symptoms subsided and his eyesight cleared, so that he could look directly through the windscreen without impaired visibility.

I only had half a lager with the others before. Surely that wouldn't affect me so badly? Phew! That was a close thing.

However, when he was feeling greatly relieved that he was back to normal, some dominant, unseen force started to filter through the principal parts of his brain. He could feel it take shape as it gave birth to itself in the cerebrum, expanding slowly into the basal ganglia and the mid-brain, embracing the cerebellum and the medulla, and finally continuing into the spinal cord itself, through the large opening in the base of his skull.

Something bad is happening here! This is really freaky.

His body felt invaded as the force flowed through his central nervous system, intent on taking complete control of his whole person.

I'm being violated. Oh no! Is it him? Randal?

Before he could cogitate some more, Marcus forgot who and where he was, as a series of jumbled messages began to unfold. A voice outlined a list of instructions for him to implement but he had to tune into the exact wavelength. He jerked his head from side to side to accommodate its requirements. He felt it was crucial to understand the demands. He could hear it all very clearly now as the other signals faded away, leaving the stage bare but for its presence.

Nothing mattered except the orders he had been given as he prepared himself for his mission. In a series of involuntary movements, like a robot on automatic pilot feeling its mechanical way on a first assignment, he sat up in his seat and put his hands on the steering wheel. He rejoined the ever-moving line of traffic but he did not see what they saw, as he sped along the road. The direction he was going in was of little relevance. What was imperative would be the authorised procedure he would carry out when he reached his final destination.

7

Clive had felt guilty that he was about to leave Randal alone in the flat on Halloween. All that afternoon, he had watched him suffer with a severe stomach upset, spending most of his time running to the toilet with agonising sickness and cramps. It was not like Randal to buckle under with an ailment but he looked ghastly, with a pale complexion and a pained expression.

"I really think I should call a doctor. It could be food poisoning you know," pointed out Clive anxiously.

"No. No, it's just a bug. I've had it before when I was a kid so I recognise the signs. It's just got to work its way out of my system. Look, don't worry about me, go out tonight and have a good time. I'll be OK," he moaned.

"How can I have a good time? Just look at you!"

"Please, I just want to rest now. What's the point of you missing out and watching me puke? I told you, I'm OK so just go."

Clive could see it was pointless arguing with him so he decided to saunter over to the party they had both been invited to. There was a strong possibility that he could bump into Marcus but there would be a large crowd and plenty of other students to hook up with.

"Right then, I'm off," reported Clive to a pale-skinned Randal as he headed for the door. "Halloween or not, if you need me just call Giles. I've left you his number by the phone. I still feel like I'm deserting a sinking ship."

Randal smiled thinly and closed his eyes.

By the time Clive got to the celebration, the place was heaving with students, mostly in fancy dress. A warlock approached him with a stunning witch at his side. It was his host, and girlfriend, Samantha.

"Hi Clive, where's the wife?" joked Samantha, about Randal's absence.

"Oh, he's got the runs or something. Tell you the truth, I nearly didn't come because he looks so bad but he insisted."

"It must be catching; Marcus isn't coming either."

Clive felt relieved and was immediately dragged into a circle of revellers, hell-bent on having a ball. Someone mentioned Randal's poem 'Halloween Dream' and how brilliant it was.

Maybe I should go back and check up on him? I can't really relax. He looked so drained. Oh God, he's always in or on my mind, one way or another.

Clive need not have worried because Randal was only feeling the after-effects of a self-induced nausea, by deliberately overdosing on laxatives. His condition was a small price to pay for the absolute privacy he needed to accomplish his most daring and challenging telepathic plan to date.

The minute Clive had left, Randal had drawn the curtains and switched off the main light, putting on a bedside lamp in its place. He was feeling a lot better than he looked. He began to prepare his unique repertoire for the evening's performance. In his hand was a coloured photograph of Marcus. It had been taken on his first visit to Clarendon Hall and was one of many he had put in his album, evolving from the same batch of negatives, which had been especially developed in anticipation of tonight's big event.

Randal studied it thoroughly and an evil expression stained his handsome features causing them to darken with ominous intent.

Right then, Master Pennington. I'll teach you to issue deceptive invitations. You need to know your place. And it isn't on this earth.

Then out of his shadowed corner, his eyes began to glow, throwing out two vivid beams of light that sliced through the dimness of the room. His gaze was so penetrative, it could have easily decimated more than one victim. He had worked out his act with split-second timing and there would be no improvisation or spontaneous fancy interfering with its perfect precision.

He had been inside Marcus's head previously, when he induced the desire for him to contact his grandfather and see him this evening. That was only a preliminary command but an essential beginning in the scheme of things. Each step was as important as the next.

As his eyes burned into the image, he re-entered Marcus's mind, just as he reached the halfway mark to Banbury. Randal felt his own hands on the steering wheel, as he caused Marcus to take the wrong turn, putting him on the road to Clarendon Hall. He needed him to collect the baggage he had hidden there, which was required in executing the climax of this very important and evil assignment.

Randal then increased the burning eye contact with the image in his hand knowing it was having a marked effect on his victim's vision. He felt a grudging respect for Marcus, as he managed to guide the car into a recessed space beside the road, regardless of his disorientation. As a reward for his dexterity in the face of such adversity, Randal had pulled out of his head for a short while.

Then, in his unequalled cruel way, just as he allowed Marcus to be lulled into a false sense of security, he moved in again for the kill. When he did, it was rapacious, infiltrating his brain and taking control of the twelve nerves passing on each side, then into the peripheral nervous system, pushing through the visceral or sympathetic system, resulting in full mental possession and total physical authority.

Randal's ownership of Marcus's faculties felt euphoric.

This feels fantastic but it's making me issue commands at breakneck speed. I'm too turned on. I'm confusing him with mumbo-jumbo messages. Slow down. Discipline is needed here with the essential telepathic delivery. Take deep breaths and don't rush. He's not going anywhere that I'm not in control of, so stick to the script and don't get carried away.

Randal's demands became more coherent. As a result, Marcus was fully tuned in to him and was now under the influence of each clear-cut instruction.

As Marcus drew nearer to Clarendon Hall, a silver Mercedes pulled alongside of him at the lights. The driver and passenger were friends of his parents. They signalled to him but he did not respond and despite repeated hand-waving and window-tapping, they failed to catch his attention. They thought he looked unusually pale and rigid in his seat, with a mechanistic posture and a robotic appearance. His eyes appeared to be glued on the road ahead.

"Young Marcus looks a bit odd. Remind me to phone Miles to see if everything's all right," said the driver.

"He does seem rather side-tracked and rigid. Not his usual jovial self at all," replied his wife.

The huge wrought-iron gates that guarded the point of entry to the Hall opened automatically as Marcus sailed through them. Randal had bypassed the security code that gave access to the main entrance and he heard the gravel crunch through Marcus's ears, as the car headed up the impressive driveway. He parked at the side of the Hall, switched off the engine and sat still, waiting for his next instruction with eager compliance.

Go to the potting shed and collect the black canvas bag, behind the spades.

Marcus opened the car door and progressed with the next imperative stage of the shared operation. It was a clear but chilly night and the full moon threw a pale spotlight over the courtyard. Marcus walked along like a mechanical figure which moved and acted as if alive, shifting spontaneously across the large paved space.

Inside the Hall, Adams had turned his head, as he glimpsed the car headlights flash across the side window as he went about his duties.

Whoever it is has breached security regulations, so it's most likely young Marcus on an unannounced visit. I'll make absolutely sure and check it all out after dinner is served.

Marcus headed for the shed. Once inside he located the canvas bag that Randal had concealed on his last visit. It was quite heavy but he picked it up effortlessly, as if it had no contents. He was oblivious to its weight, only his intention to convey it safely to his final port of call. He walked back to the car and put it into the boot. Then he drove out of the grounds and linked up again with the country road.

Randal looked smugly demonic in the confines of his room and smiled affectedly.

So far, so good. This is going well. The Right Reverend Leslie Stainthorpe, here we come.

As Marcus drove round the final bend that would take him to his grandfather's rectory, Randal felt the adrenaline pump through his veins, making his pulse points throb with an almost unbearable excitement. He seemed to produce an electric field around him, raising him above his ground state; almost like a molecule that was capable of existing independently with all its properties.

Marcus felt the rush of violent activity shoot through him by proxy, as he pressed his foot down hard on the accelerator to increase his rate of motion.

The Reverend looked at his watch and at the same time, the grandfather clock in the hallway chimed eight. *Marcus should be here any moment now*, he thought, as he walked into the kitchen to put the kettle on. One of his parishioners had baked him a fruitcake which would make an ideal accompaniment to a pot of tea for two. He cut a section of it into four thick slices and arranged them on a bone china plate, which usually took centre stage in his late mother's Welsh dresser. It was part of an expensive service but tonight he would utilise it to entertain his eldest grandson. He was just putting some milk in a matching jug when he heard the bell ring.

He opened the door to find Marcus stood on its step and Leslie was so pleased to see him that he did not notice the peculiar, manufactured smile which looked like a stretched gash across his face. He greeted him warmly, putting an arm around his shoulder as he welcomed him inside.

"Marcus my dear boy! I'm so glad to see you. Come on in, out of the cold," he enthused in a hospitable manner.

"Thanks, Gramps," replied Marcus, as he heard Randal's voice telling him to act perfectly normal.

"What's in the bag?" asked Leslie when he saw the holdall he was carrying.

"Just notes and stuff from my English syllabus," answered Marcus casually.

"Well bring it inside. You can look at it later. I'm in the middle of making us some tea with your favourite cake. I'll be with you in a jiffy. Make yourself comfortable."

Marcus nodded. Randal moved inside him and surveyed the surroundings through his eyes. His gaze was drawn to the religious artefacts that were dotted around the room. A huge crucifix adorned one wall and Randal quickly averted his eyes away from its holy aura. There were two original paintings of devout priests above the mantelpiece and a bookcase crammed with biblical reading matter to its left. The overwhelming sense of piety and worship was suffocating and only made Randal even more impatient to rid himself of its ornamentation.

When Leslie returned with refreshments, Marcus was seated on an old comfortable armchair, flicking through the pages of a magazine.

"Here we are then. I'm glad you've called round tonight. I was feeling a little sad about this Sunday's sermon; not long now until I retire. My replacement is very commendable and he's the perfect choice for our church. Younger and sprightlier, I dare say."

Marcus just kept turning the pages in the periodical.

"It doesn't seem that long ago that I was ordained and now, here I am, at the end of my run, so to speak," Leslie sighed as he poured out the tea.

Marcus still carried on rotating the sheets of paper.

"I'm not boring you, am I?" queried Leslie, when he seemed to be doing all of the talking with no response but before Marcus could reply, the telephone rang in the hall and Leslie excused himself as he left the room to answer it.

Randal was impatient to set the ball rolling and here was an unexpected opportunity. There was no need for delaying tactics and as soon as Leslie departed, he spoke to Marcus telepathically.

Go and look inside the bag and you'll see a large piece of blue cloth. Take it out, unwrap it carefully and you'll find a gun. Also, there are two separate lengths of rope. Bring one of them out and leave the other intact. Close the bag and put the gun under your sweatshirt. Go back to your seat and conceal the rope behind you. Now wait for your next instruction.

Marcus carried out his orders with unquestioning obedience. Eventually Leslie returned after a long telephone call, apologising for the interruption.

"Church business," he sighed "there's always something or other to see to. Now, where were we?"

Marcus looked peculiar. His eyes had a glazed expression in them and the pupils were both hugely dilated. His skin colour had paled and he was in a trance. Leslie frowned deeply. He hoped that Marcus had not taken some mind-altering drug that so many young people were experimenting with these days. He knew of the dangers because he had counselled some of their parents, who had turned to him in desperation when all else was lost.

"Are you all right, Marcus? You've not touched your tea or cake," he observed with great concern.

Marcus did not reply and stared into an empty space. Then very, very slowly he turned his eyes towards his grandfather but his expression was unreadable.

"Marcus, what's wrong with you? Are you on drugs?" asked Leslie, as he got out of his chair to approach him.

"Sit down, old man!" ordered Marcus. In Randal's voice.

Leslie's skin began to crawl. That was not his grandson who had just spoken. He could not move and stood rooted to the spot.

"I said, sit down!" snarled Marcus and this time Leslie knew for sure.

It was Randal. Beyond any shadow of a doubt. He was here in the room, living and breathing through Marcus. Leslie fell back into the chair and his mouth dropped open as Marcus brought out the gun from under his shirt and pointed it in his direction. It was the pistol that Randal had stolen from the gun room at Clarendon while the ever-ready Lady Pennington was bathing, after their last steamy session.

Leslie recognised it instantly and knew its removal was not the work of Marcus. He was being driven by a devil in human form; a demon who preyed on the righteous and left a trail of unwholesome destruction behind him. A fiend who would use whoever he wished to do his evil bidding.

Marcus had been right all along and the proof of his theory was standing right in front of him, breathing its demonic life force into the host body of his vulnerable and beloved grandson.

"What do you want?" whispered Leslie, mustering up every ounce of courage he had through the power of his faith.

"You! I want you!" laughed Marcus cruelly, as he walked towards his grandfather, gun in one hand and a length of thick, twisted cord in the other.

Leslie's eyes widened with fear. *Dear Lord, if you can hear me, then please help us*, he pleaded inwardly but Randal heard his invocation.

"Praying won't get you anywhere, old man. People like you never learn, do you?"

Marcus stretched out the loaded firearm towards Leslie as Randal continued to speak through him.

"You dabble with subjects that are way beyond your puny, human comprehension. You meddle in things that are ten thousand light years away from your mental grasp. You presume; you convict; you conspire; you deduct. But worst of all, you decide! And what do you decide? A bloody useless, old-fashioned exorcism to rid the world of all the so-called devil's disciples. Don't you?"

Marcus sneered, holding the gun against Leslie's forehead.

"I SAID DON'T YOU!" he shouted down his ear and Leslie found himself nodding repeatedly as he felt the cold, hard metal pressing against his right temple.

"Well then, Right Reverend Leslie Stainthorpe. Should I tell you what I've decided?"

Leslie swallowed hard and from somewhere at the back of his throat, he found his voice.

"No! No Marcus! I don't want to know what you've decided because it's what Randal's decided for you! Listen to me! You can fight this! I'll help you with every last breath in my body! You must cast this evil presence out! CAST HIM OUT! You don't have to obey him! He's all you said he is! Look inside yourself and find the real you! Randal Forbes is using you. You were right. I should have listened to you. We can fight him together. Search deeply inside your mind. He's powerless if you ignore him. DON'T LISTEN TO HIS WORDS!" cried Leslie, desperate for his advice to sink into Marcus's brain.

Randal felt Marcus begin to pull away from him. He had to give him some credit. The old priest had struck a holy chord in his subconscious and he was struggling to respond. Now he simply had no choice but to increase his hold over him. This had never happened before and the infusion could prove fatal if too powerful but he would have to take the chance if Marcus was going to complete his mission. Randal concentrated harder and activated a further violent and dangerous abduction of Marcus's senses. Leslie saw the struggle on his grandson's face as he fought its rampant violation, only to be overcome by its powerful ownership.

And all resistance crumbled away as Randal's gamble paid off and he took sole possession once more.

The immense effort had depleted Randal's store of reserve energy and could possibly take its toll on his telepathic powers of control. He could not afford to prolong his victim's agony in any way and certainly would not be allowed to wallow in the usual sadistic pleasure each psychic murder gave him. The whole plan had to be completed in both a quick and clean manner, with none of the demonic fringe benefits. He spoke again through Marcus, issuing his commands with firm authorisation.

"Now keep very still or else I'll make this quick and just shoot you stone dead."

Marcus picked up the length of rope and proceeded to tie up his grandfather. He knotted his hands and feet together and then continued to encircle him, restricting his freedom of movement entirely, by binding the cord around his body. Finally, he secured him to the chair itself, by which time Leslie knew he was doomed. This still did not stop him from urging Marcus to look deep inside his head and realise what was happening to him. He begged and pleaded continuously, but his requests were ignored, as Marcus dipped once more inside the black bag and brought out a container, then disappeared with it into the hallway.

Leslie held his breath and began to tremble with anticipation. He listened anxiously for any movement and heard a splashing sound coming from just outside the door. He was puzzled momentarily and then it hit him like an ill-omened realisation, as he sniffed the unmistakable smell of kerosene. Marcus came back into the room, juggling with the weight of the plastic container, as he purposefully soaked everything around them, with huge puddles of paraffin oil.

Leslie felt real panic rise up inside him.

"HELP US! PLEASE HELP US!" he shouted in the vain hope that there was someone in earshot.

He paused to cough as the petrol fumes settled on his chest. The more he yelled, the more Marcus saturated the furniture and fittings, until every last drop of oil had been emptied.

"You vile and filthy abomination!" spluttered the Reverend. "This vengeance is for nothing! Marcus and I didn't want anything to do with you. He was always afraid of you; really afraid of what you might do to our family and because of that, I turned my back on it all. I should have believed him sooner. I never should have let it get this far. I should have put him off right from the very start and just told him to stay well away from you. Do you ever listen to the pleas of your victims, Randal Forbes? Or give them a fair trial? I never wanted to destroy you. I just wanted to redeem your soul!"

Leslie choked, fighting for every breath.

Marcus reached inside the bag for the last time. In his hand he held a box of matches and he opened it to take one out.

"Do you know what tonight is, old man?"

Marcus's eyes looked possessed as he totally disregarded the priest's passionate line of defence.

Leslie coughed persistently and could not answer him.

"You don't know? Well let me enlighten you. Tonight, my dear Right Reverend Stainthorpe, is Halloween. And do you know what your fellow priests used to do in days of old to all those so-called witches?

I'm sure you do really but let me take this opportunity to remind you. They burned them at the stake. Tut, tut. Can you believe such primeval behaviour? Well tonight I'm going to reverse the penalty. I'm their dark avenging attendant spirit. Can you guess how? Hmm?"

Leslie began to recite the Lord's Prayer as Marcus picked up the remaining length of rope then struck the match and threw it on the floor a few yards away. It ignited instantly in a roaring sea of flames which spread like wildfire all around causing instant devastation.

"Holier than thou until the very end. Give my warmest regards to the rest of the fallen angels, won't you?"

Marcus ran out of the building before the fire blocked his exit point. The burning matter swept quickly towards his grandfather, who began to suffocate as the carbon particles of smoke filled up his lungs. He felt himself blacking out but before he did, he continued to pray for his grandson's divine redemption and the sanctification of his desecrated soul.

From a safe distance outside, Marcus watched the conflagration destroy everything in its path. Windowpanes were blown out and smashed to smithereens, as sharp glazed sprays flew through the air, covering the garden in a blanket of splintered glass.

At the bottom of the lawn stood a large oak tree that Marcus used to climb as a child. He had built a tree house there with his sister, Felicity, and they had resided in their own world of imagination in its leafy boughs. Those long, hot days of summers past had always remained in his mind; the eternal desire to return to the uncomplicated security of his childhood, where life was one lingering holiday of parental love and adolescent dreams.

It was here that Randal led him in order to complete the final stage of the whole operation. Marcus found himself staring at the mighty oak. He could feel the intense heat of the fire behind him, although he was well away from it. The full moon was partially hidden by its huge ancient boughs which branched out from the great breadth of its bark. He began to climb, shinning up its thick, gnarled trunk with the second length of rope slung over his shoulder. When he reached a certain height, he crawled forward on one of the strong, protruding branches to his left. He stopped halfway to tie the rope around it, pulling at the knot to make sure it was secure.

When he was satisfied, he let go of the rest, watching it fall and dangle above the marble birdbath. He made his way back down to the ground and walked over to the loose end of cord. It was still swaying from its recent drop. He clambered on to the marble pedestal and shaped the end of the rope into a noose, checking that its loop made a running knot which would tighten as the chord was pulled. When he was satisfied with the result, he reached out to place it around his neck. The vertical alignment between the birdbath and the noose itself was perfect.

Marcus jumped and Randal congratulated himself on such faultless precision.

By this time the raging fire had been spotted in the vicinity. Although the rectory was set back off the road, in its own large grounds, the bright blaze of burning matter and the dense, dark smoke could easily be seen. A few of the locals reported it to the emergency services and a growing crowd of people was gathering nearby. They addressed each other anxiously, greatly alarmed as to the whereabouts of their parish priest. One man wanted to go and investigate but was held back by the others who said that the fire was far too fierce for them to get any closer.

"It's too dangerous so leave it to the experts. They're on their way; I've been assured."

"Yes, but someone should contact Lady Pennington. Her father's in great danger."

"She should be informed right away!" shouted another anxious voice.

They all agreed but before anyone could do so, the wailing sirens of the fire engines could be heard tearing up the road. The two heavily equipped vehicles with their pumps and ladders sped towards the burning building and pulled up outside the gates.

"Is there anybody in there that you know of?" asked one fireman as he jumped down out of the cab.

"We're not too sure if Reverend Stainthorpe, our parish priest, is actually at home. He sometimes visits his family. They own Clarendon Hall. His daughter is Lady Pennington."

"Right then, first things first," he concluded as he organised his men to carry out their duties.

The gateway to the rectory was far too narrow for them to drive through but in no time at all, they had unloaded their equipment and pointed their fire hoses towards the heart of the blaze. Several powerful jets of water gushed out of each long, flexible pipe, which stretched the whole length of the drive.

They all worked tirelessly together to extinguish the glowing mass of burning matter which spat and crackled mercilessly to disturb the tranquillity of the night. Another team of firemen went around the back of the property to tackle the blaze but it was too ferocious, making any rescue attempt very perilous. They tried to climb through the broken windows but were beaten back by a vigorous sea of flames, equally as hot as any molten volcanic rock, bubbling under the earth's crust.

One of the men saw an unspecified object run past him on the ground. He looked closer and saw it was a frightened tortoiseshell cat, fleeing in confusion, to the bottom of the lawn where it scampered up the oak tree to safety.

Something else caught his eye. At first, he thought it was a pair of trousers dangling on a washing line. It was hard to distinguish its shape accurately through all the smoke so he moved nearer, screwing up his eyes in the semi-darkness, as he tried to focus in on it.

Halfway down the garden he knew exactly what it was and felt the shockwaves of his gruesome discovery flow through him.

He shouted out for assistance but there was too much chaos behind him for anyone to hear his cries. He ran back to the fire engine, looking for his superior and pulled him away from the frantic scene.

"Chief! Chief! I think you better come and see this!" he urged, looking visibly shaken.

He led him to the tree and when they looked up at Marcus, his head was drooped to one side and his wide, unblinking eyes stared straight into nowhere.

"Is he dead?" asked the young fireman.

"No, he's hanging around for a lift. Of course he's dead, you clown," replied his chief sarcastically.

"What should we do?"

"Fetch the law! NOW!" he shouted with authority and his fellow team member jumped to attention.

Contact was swiftly made and the police arrived very shortly afterwards. All of the onlookers were still in the dark about the events. Then another car pulled up with a detective inspector and speculation was rife that they had found the body of the Reverend inside the building. One more vehicle had been permanently parked on the opposite side of the road, across from the rectory. It was eventually identified by its registration and tax disc.

"Does anyone know Marcus Pennington?" asked the detective to the ever-increasing crowd.

"He's the Reverend's grandson," a woman informed them, "Oh God, don't tell us that he's inside there as well? He must have been visiting his grandfather. Oh, this is too terrible for words."

At the bottom of the garden they had cut Marcus down. They removed the rope from around his neck and laid him to rest on the ground. They searched around for any clues but found nothing. Then suddenly, to their utter amazement, they heard him whimper. The Inspector examined him and felt a faint pulse in his wrist.

"Call an ambulance!" he instructed loudly as the moaning grew louder.

Marcus moved his head fractionally and tried to swallow with tremendous effort. A deep red friction burn ran angrily around the circumference of his neck, where the rope had dug into his flesh. He opened and closed his mouth like a goldfish in a fairground bowl. Not one word came out.

"It's all right, son, don't try to speak," comforted one of the policemen on the scene but Marcus could not hear him. "It's all right. You're not alone."

Behind them the fire still raged on. This was one Halloween that the local townsfolk of Banbury would not forget in a hurry.

And back in Oxford, in the sinister shadows of his room, Randal awarded himself an Oscar for his best production to date.

Randal looked bloodless as he lay naked on his ruffled bed. The crumpled photograph of Marcus had fallen on to the floor, next to a pair of Clive's socks that had seen better days. Randal moaned and covered his burning eyes with his hands, their lashes scorched from the continual heat of his penetrative gaze. His face and body glistened with a saturated film of perspiration and he felt completely drained. Never in the whole of his young life had he been so spiritually or physically exhausted. Additionally, a malaise had kicked in with the anticlimax, after hours of plotting and scheming for tonight's big event.

Although Randal had patted himself on the back for a spectacular result, Marcus had proved to be much more difficult to manipulate than he had envisaged. It had not been a total walkover, largely due to the old priest's endeavours to thwart Randal's possession. His faith had been very strong and he had almost succeeded. The extra effort needed to recharge his telepathic hold over the situation, plus the amount of time taken to complete the whole operation, had taken its toll on Randal's well-being. He felt ghastly.

Where the hell's Clive? I wish he'd come back right now. I'm not used to feeling my mortality. I'm like all the other lesser mortals who call upon their strength and vitality to cope with a crisis. They rise to the occasion and then after the event they feel cream-crackered when the moment of danger or difficulty has passed. I'm far from happy with the similarity. I thought I was way above such crap. I guess I'm part human after all. Clive! Please come back! I'm too wiped out to contact you.

At the very end of the operation when Marcus was climbing up the tree to secure the rope, Randal had decided to change the plot. Due to his passion for Fiona, he would save her son's miserable soul by leaving the noose a little slack, so that when he hanged himself, the stranglehold would be just a small degree below the tightness required to kill him. But Marcus would have to pay a very high price for his clemency.

Randal had wiped his memory banks clean, eliminating all recollection of his life at Beaumont College. Marcus would not be able to recognise any of his new-found friends and his life at Oxford would be a blank page. His larynx, regardless of its protection in front by cartilages, would be permanently damaged. His vocal chords would cease to vibrate and produce sound, making speech impossible.

Randal's savagery cut through his debilitated state and invaded his thoughts.

Marcus, old foe. You'll never be able to recall anything leading up to the fire or the reason why you were there in the first place. Evidence, like the smell of kerosene on your hands and clothes, will point towards your guilt but your daddy will no doubt employ an eminent barrister to exonerate you with a plea of diminished responsibility. And that's about it. You're finished. Over. Redundant. Caput. That'll teach you and your saintly grandfather to try and analyse 'the gift' and issue fraudulent invitations to unearth my benefaction.

The tragic death of her father and the psychiatric incarceration of her son would initially leave Fiona Pennington devastated. Randal knew that. But he dismissed it.

Don't fret, my sweet siren of the manor. You'll come to terms with it all one day but in the foreseeable future, I'll be there for you, whenever you need me. You can rely on me to keep your bed warm and soothe away your pain. Look upon me as an incestuous stand-in for your son. I'll willingly take Marcus's place. Milady.

8

Dottie gave birth to a baby girl in June 1978. They called her Shannon, after the river of the same name, because Neil was positive that she had been conceived in Ireland, the previous autumn. Randal and Clive had just completed their second year at Beaumont and had driven home together on the spur of the moment to Chester. Randal was pleased for his Aunty Dottie, but mostly for Dean, who had been deprived of his real father's bloodline. He contemplated.

Somewhere, Dean, in this unworthy world, you've got two half-sisters but now Shannon will fill the tainted gaps in the depleted Sterling-free family tree.

There was a large gathering at Dottie's and Neil's house by the time they arrived. They had set out early from Oxford in Randal's car, taking turns at the wheel and stopping just once at a motorway service station for a coffee and a sandwich. They arrived in Chester at the newly built property, with its double driveway and extensive gardens, which was situated close to Neil's law firm and fitting in style for a solicitor of his standing.

Randal parked the car and walked ahead of Clive with long, loose strides, rather similar in style to his father's gait. Margaret was sat on one of the window seats in the front room and spotted him as he approached the front door. Her handsome little boy was now a smouldering, first-class example of modern masculinity and she gave herself a mental pat on the back for producing such a prize. She was still as blind to his dark exploits as she had always been. All she saw was his amazing aura and tantalising allure, which set him entirely apart from the rest.

"Randal's here!" she confirmed excitedly to Edward, as the doorbell rang.

"Oh great!" exclaimed Patricia who was sat in the corner near her mother. She jumped up out of her seat to greet him.

There were some of Neil's family in the hallway and Patricia flew in between them to embrace Randal, as he stepped over the threshold.

"Whoa! I know I'm irresistible, sis, but let me come in!" he joked immodestly, as she hugged and kissed him repeatedly.

"What about little old me? Don't I count?" piped up Clive, making his bottom lip wobble.

"Oh Clive! Hi, sorry but I didn't see you behind Randal," she smiled widely and gave him a peck on his cheek.

They're still glued together. A couple or just friends? Alison must be blind.

As Randal shook hands with everyone, Patricia watched their reaction to his presence. Her eyes roamed over his copper-red hair and handsome face, down to the pale blue jacket and jeans and she found herself wishing she was not his sister.

Look at the effect he's having upon all the women. He's so hot! Brother or no brother! What chance has Alison got? She's got her work cut out. A walking, talking sex bomb!

Randal picked up on her thoughts and smiled knowingly, as he continued to greet the guests, who were still blocking his and Clive's access into the lounge. Patricia had just completed her first year at university and had no shortage of male admirers. She looked and acted very much like her Aunty Dottie had at her age, with the same silky fair hair, blue eyes, pretty face, long legs and outgoing personality. Watching Randal weaving and charming his way through the crowd, Patricia realised why none of her boyfriends had ever come up to scratch.

I'm comparing them all to Randal. He's magical and they're so ordinary. Perhaps Robbie Sterling would have run him a close second. There was something about him too, but now I'll never know. So very sad. Poor Robbie.

She saw their mother's face light up as Randal made his way over to her. She was still besotted by his magnetism and their father had much the same expression as he clasped Randal's hand in his own.

Clive was greeted kindly after the fuss of Randal's unexpected appearance. He was used to playing second fiddle to the maestro. As long as he had exclusive possession he would cope. Besides, he actually enjoyed seeing the effect Randal had upon the masses and felt in a position of superiority, simply by being his closest subordinate.

Clive knew that Randal had been entirely responsible for last year's Halloween devastation involving Marcus and his grandfather. He had managed to lock the harrowing event away, in the deepest, concealed corners of his mind. He had not agonised over it all, as he had done with Robbie's death, because he would have made himself ill again. When he returned to the flat from the party, that fateful night, he had found Randal sprawled naked on the bed, in a state of outright collapse. The room felt cold but Randal was flushed and red hot, the sweat sliding feverishly down his body. Clive had rushed to his side.

"Look at you! Just look at you! You're worse than when I left! I'm calling a doctor right now!"

"No, I'm OK. Believe me… it's not what you think. I've had to… well I've had to… had to see to a few things… that were bothering me," Randal struggled to reply, his breathing somewhat laboured.

"What things? What fucking things! Don't tell me you've been out in your state!" exclaimed Clive.

"No… not out exactly. At least not… physically," panted Randal, the skin on his bare chest glistening in the semi-darkness.

Clive shook his head with disbelief.

"Just what do you mean? I should never have gone to that stupid party and left you alone!"

Clive caught sight of Marcus's scrunched-up image on the floor and bent down to pick it up for closer inspection. He opened out the creased photograph and studied it for a moment or two. He lifted his gaze towards Randal and their eyes locked together.

Not one word passed between them but Clive knew. He did not want to hear any of the grim details. Judging by the condition Randal was in, it must have been a long, drawn-out sequence; another act of unspeakable, horrendous revenge.

"Do you want a drink of water?" was all Clive said, stroking Randal's damp hair off his stunning face in a loving gesture.

Randal nodded. Clive covered him over with the top sheet which had been thrown back along with the blankets at the foot of his bed.

"You can't lie here naked. Even though you're sweating you'll still catch cold."

Randal sipped slowly out of the glass as Clive held his head. He was still fighting for breath but the crisis point was behind him. Throughout the night Clive held him in the reassuring circle of his arms as he slept, continually wiping down his face and body with a towel. This was the very first time that Clive had accepted the re-emergence of 'the gift' without recrimination. His main concern was for his idol, not for his targeted victim. Clive had gladly sacrificed his own sleep in order to keep a vigil over his debilitated lover, even though he had an important tutorial in the morning; the same one Marcus would have had.

Oh Lord! What's he done to him? I'm dreading hearing about it.

Before the end of the next afternoon, the news about Marcus had ripped through the college walls like a veritable forest fire; a grotesque, giant tinderbox of tragedy.

"Who'd have believed a cool dude like Pennington would want to bump off his grandfather by setting fire to his rectory and then try to top himself? It's unreal!" gulped one of his crowd, visibly upset by the whole issue.

Clive ran away from the endless gossip. His head was pounding and he felt sick with an overwhelming sense of guilt and shame. He rushed outside to take a few deep breaths of fresh air, projectile-vomited and then leaned against the wall for support.

No wonder you were so wiped out. Well you've certainly surpassed yourself this time. Even for you! Even for you!

Clive quaked inwardly, feeling a sudden desire to sprint out of the grounds and never stop running.

There followed several police enquiries. Quite a number of students had been quizzed over their relationship with Marcus. Clive and Randal were called in separately for questioning and Clive was enormously relieved that he was not in the same room, when they pumped him for possible answers.

The only thing that was unearthed was Marcus's same-sex relationships.

"We've got nothing to go on really," said the detective inspector in charge, "I think that young Pennington visited the Reverend and they rowed about his sexual preference. He was obviously a closet depressive as well, so in a disturbed state of mind, he set fire to the building and killed his grandfather unintentionally. Then when he realised what he'd done, he tried to take his own life. It looks like a clear-cut case of manslaughter with diminished responsibility but we'll let the court decide."

Clive came back into the present as the voices around him woke him out of his unwanted, dire recollection. Randal had disappeared into the kitchen, where Dean was talking to their grandmother, Emily. Neither of them was aware of his presence in the house. Dean loved his new baby sister but all the fuss over her arrival was becoming tiresome. Emily sensed Dean's growing unrest and had purposefully gone out of her way to give him that extra attention. He was just telling her about his school friend when Randal walked in on their conversation.

"What's new then? Anything I should know about?" he said smiling; that famous irresistible smile.

"Randal, oh wow!" squealed Dean, his boredom forgotten as he saw his favourite cousin in the doorway and bolted into his arms.

Randal winked at his grandmother as Dean held him tightly. Emily was very impressed by her eldest grandson and felt a sense of inner pride at the way he had turned out.

He really is the most handsome young man. So brilliant and charming.

Dean was still hanging on to his shirt tails as Randal approached his grandmother.

"Hi, Gran! I thought I'd surprise everyone by just turning up. It's a good chance to be with you all again. Seems ages since I last saw you," he said softly, kissing her cheek with genuine affection.

"It is! It's almost a year, Randal," she scolded half-heartedly. "You didn't come home for Christmas and we were all looking forward to seeing you; your mother especially. She was very upset. Naughty boy."

"I know, I know, it was wrong of me. I just got caught up with parties and stuff in Oxford. It's no excuse but I do lose track of the time. So much to do, you see. That's why I tried hard to make it here today. Will you forgive me?" he asked in an old-fashioned manner, going down on one knee and kissing her hand.

Sorry, Gran, but the Lady of the Hall invited me round for dinner and a dalliance. She's devastated about the old priest and Marcus, so

I had to sacrifice my own trip home to help her cope. She was very accommodating considering her loss.

He looked up at his grandmother through his unruly fringe and Emily saw the child he had once been in his appealing expression. She laughed out loud at his transparent charm in what was obviously a staged attempt to win her over. She could never refuse him anything when he was in this mood and he knew it.

Dean was still tugging furiously at his arm to follow him upstairs where he was dying to show Randal his latest model aeroplane.

"Soon, Dean, just let me speak to Grandma for a while and then we'll go. OK?" he said, ruffling his cousin's hair.

Dean nodded and then listened in awe as Randal wove a magical spell around them. The bond was stronger than ever and Dean thought that when he was older, he would work with Randal, so that their lives would be permanently intertwined.

When the party was over, Randal dropped Clive off at his house and then went back home to Didsbury. He excused himself to the family and retired to bed early. He was shattered from his drive and the previous weeks of studying, wild socialising, Clive-clinging, Alison-allocating and Fiona-fornicating.

The next day he felt a renewed vigour, as if all his depleted cells had been replaced with forcible ones. This rejuvenation was not just a physical thing. His spirit had also been recharged, reviving him with a sense of familiar immortality. He had not told his family that he had recently finalised a trip to Mexico with Clive because they still had two months of free time before they embarked on their final year at Beaumont College.

Mum will freak. I'll tell her over breakfast. It's not what she wants but I have to go.

He had told his publishers to expect a novel by the end of the year. Although he already had one successful book of poetry, he had not attempted a complete work of fiction. They had made allowances for him because he was still a student and working towards a degree but they also knew that his talent was limitless and were prepared to wait for his next creation. When he informed them that he was writing a fictional story with a Mexican theme, and needed to fly out there to research, they were willing to advance him the money to cover his expenses.

"I want you with me," said Randal to Clive. "You can help me with the book; jot down my ideas and even smack them into shape. What do you say?"

"I say yes, yes, and yes," enthused Clive, his heart beating fast at the whole idea of working and sleeping with his icon. It would be a complete Randalisation, with an exciting project thrown in. Perfection personified.

Somewhere between the mind-crunching layers of his literary inventions, Randal had a need for the chosen few. So far, Alison, Clive and Dean were at the forefront, together with his parents, sister and certain extended family. His past nanny, Victoria, was in the running and more recently he had added Lady Pennington to the list. He knew his followers and they would be considered respectively.

Back in the present, Margaret was excited to have her children around her. She fussed over them and they let her, even though they were quite capable of serving themselves. Edward smiled to himself.

Just look at her luxuriating in her maternal role. The children are only on loan for a few months but she's making the most of the time we're all together as a family; must admit that I'm more than happy to have them back. Even for a short while.

Randal finished his toast and jam and poured himself another cup of tea, wiping the crumbs away from his mouth with a paper napkin.

"I've got something to tell you. Now, Mum, don't get upset but I'm going to Mexico next week to do some research for my latest book. It's a fantastic opportunity."

"Mexico! But you've only just come home for the summer! Can't you stay a little longer? There's so much to talk about, Randal. We never got a chance to see you last Christmas and now you're off again!" complained Margaret forlornly, as Randal smiled at her and touched her cheek affectionately.

"I know, Mum, but it's really important that I go. I need to soak up the atmosphere and see all the sights for myself, for at least a month. Anyway, we'll still have one whole week together before I fly out and I promise to spend every day with you. OK?" he said gently, still stroking her face.

"You'll be away for at least a month!" she wailed. She wanted to pump him about all sorts of things, so she fired questions at him one after the other.

"Margaret, for heaven's sake; give the boy a chance to explain," scolded Edward, as she interrupted Randal's reply to her former query, by asking him another one.

"Don't you dare lecture me for caring about our son! This is the first time in ages that he's sat at our table. I can't help my curiosity, can I?" she criticised indignantly.

Randal laughed inwardly at his mother's expression as she looked sternly at his father for admonishing her.

She idolises me. Each word that comes out of my mouth is a precious pearl. Having me home is a rarity. She just wants to discover everything all at once. I do love her. In my own way.

"What do you want to know, Mum? I'm all yours," he smiled, holding her hand.

"Your father thinks I'm being too inquisitive," she protested.

"I never said that," contradicted Edward. "I just thought you should give him time to answer each question fully. It's common courtesy."

Margaret opened her mouth to disagree but Randal intercepted their discourse.

"Clive's coming with me," he said, changing the subject.

"Clive?" repeated Patricia questioningly.

"Yes. He with the ginger thatch of halo-hair, and freckled face; the one who was with us yesterday," replied Randal sarcastically. "It'll be me, him and Mexico City."

"Oh, I'm so glad," enthused Margaret, missing his mocking tone. "I was worried about you travelling alone. I can't think of anyone better to go with."

"What about Alison?" cross-examined Patricia. "Will she be joining you as well?"

"No, I shouldn't think so, she's far too busy touring," answered Randal through narrowed eyes, picking up on his sister's suspicious curiosity.

"I see," she said as she filled her teacup again.

Randal looked inside her head. He saw a past image of him and Clive in a close embrace in his bedroom.

When did she see us like that? It must be ages ago. She's said nothing.

"Do you want to come with us? You can if you want. Clive won't mind," lied Randal.

"Won't he? I'm sure he doesn't want your little sister trailing around in the Aztec rubble. It's tempting but I'll give it a miss. Anyway, I'm going to France with my friend, Sally, but thanks for asking me," she said politely with a knowing smile.

Randal knew that her lips were sealed. Anyway, it was a while ago when she saw him and Clive touching each other up, and as he was going to ask Alison to be his wife, the subject would just be part of his adolescent past. His admiration for his sister's discretion went up several notches. He would soon get around her with his charisma. She would forget it ever happened.

They all carried on conversing and inevitably the subject of Marcus and his grandfather was eventually raised.

"How are the Penningtons? Have you heard from them, Randal?" asked Margaret cautiously.

"Not so good, Mum. It's had a lasting affect on them, especially Lady Pennington. She's quite devastated."

"I should think she is. It's hard enough losing her father but her son's part in it all must have really sent her over the edge. How dreadful. It doesn't even bear thinking about," shuddered Margaret.

"Marcus is more to be pitied. It was some form of acute psychological disturbance and he'll pay the price for his actions all his life. I don't just mean his incarceration but his guilt and remorse," replied Randal with false empathy.

"I think you're being somewhat magnanimous, Randal. He must have known what he was doing regardless of his anger towards his grandfather for finding out he was homosexual. At least that was the reason for his crime given by the Oxford constabulary in the newspaper report. I feel so sorry for his parents. It's beyond words," added Margaret.

"I've no time whatsoever for his kind. I think it's unnatural and immoral," lectured Edward disgustedly and Patricia pulled a face.

"Oh Daddy, don't be so prejudiced. They are as they are. It's perfectly natural for them. Any kind of love is better than hatred. Anyway, you can't possibly be so judgemental without knowing the people involved," Patricia upbraided.

Randal knew that his father was stuck in his heterosexual bubble but he still smiled inwardly to himself.

Patricia's cottoned on but the others haven't a clue. How can a family of such high calibre be so duped? As for my mother, if she was to see me Clive-seducing, eyes-flaring and evil-deeds-deeding, right in front of her, she would still convince herself of my innocence.

"To tell you the truth, Randal, I was really worried about your state of mind over Marcus, especially coming so soon after Robbie's death," added Edward, raking up unwanted emotions for both Margaret and Patricia. Randal cursed inwardly.

Here we go. Now back to the Sterling saga. Get ready for another inquisition.

Patricia felt a shiver run down her spine as her father raked up the ashes of her never-to-be-had love affair with

Robbie. Even though his death had been an accident, or so she believed, it was such a waste of life. The Marcus Pennington chronicle was also a tragic story with another horrendous ending. Both of them had been vibrant young men in the prime of their lives. Now Robbie was dead and Marcus had to live in a huge, painful vacuum of memory loss and guilt over his grandfather's demise. She pushed her plate to one side and stood up.

"Let's not talk about all this depressing news. There's nothing any of us can do to change the outcome," advised Patricia, as her eyes filled up with unshed tears; the sadness spread over her pretty face, creasing her features into a crumpled version of their usual form. She looked like her Aunty Dottie.

"You OK, blondie? Come here and give me a hug," soothed Randal, as he got up from the table.

She fell into his strong arms and felt secure. She loved him so much and he knew it.

You're better off without that son of a slimy toad. I'll keep you safe until you find the right guy and eliminate those who aren't fit to kiss your feet. I know what's best for you and it wasn't Robbie 'Shithead' Sterling. Trust me.

"You said in your last phone call that you were going to Clarendon Hall. Do you go there often, Randal?" asked Margaret.

Then he told them all about his visits, describing in great detail the beauty of the manor and the hospitality he had always received but skirting around the real reason for his return trips. Since the fire, he had been back to comfort Fiona once a week and she had welcomed his red-hot passion with open arms and legs.

Marcus had been very ill and was in a private sanatorium for the criminally insane where he was receiving all the constant medical attention money could buy. Although his laryngitis was painful to live with, it was his mental condition that drove him to the brink of insanity. Marcus's mother still craved Randal's touch and needed it to take her mind off the bleak reality of her present situation.

Margaret sipped at her tea and felt enormous misplaced respect for Fiona, even though she had never met her.

"I can't tell you how much admiration I have for Lady Pennington. She still leaves the door open for her son's friend to call. If I were her, I'd want to hide away. She must think a lot of you, Randal. Not that I blame her. You'd light up the darkest room," she said adoringly.

Randal smiled his special smile. *Oh, Mother, if only you knew.*

Edward marvelled at Randal's maturity. Patricia felt fortunate to have the emotional security that her brother provided. They all knew that Randal was very different from the crowd but they did not realise the true extent of that dissimilarity.

Randal had moulded them into a hoodwinked trio of followers. None of them had ever seen the darkness around him and they would spit feathers at anyone who would demagnetise his attributes.

★★★

Randal spent the next week in the company of his parents, especially his mother's. She was enjoying every precious moment of their time together. One day, she had taken him shopping in Wilmslow, to an exclusive gents' outfitters for some new clothes, which she thought would be ideal for his trip abroad.

"Mum, you're not paying for all this," he said when he saw the expensive price tags.

"It's my absolute pleasure, so shush," she replied affectionately.

She had been very generous and had purchased some cool cotton trousers and shorts; four pure silk shirts in varying pastel shades; an exclusive pair of brown leather sandals and two wide-brimmed hats to protect his head in the heat of the Mexican sun.

Randal kept darting in and out of the changing room to show her how he looked in each garment and she could not help but compare him to some of the other customers. Beside her son, they all looked plain and insignificant.

"Have you ever thought of modelling?" asked a male assistant, as Randal paraded up and down in white cotton trousers, a pale green shirt and a straw hat.

"Why? Do you think I'd pass?" he replied with a dazzling smile.

Margaret laughed out loud at his false modesty and Randal tipped his sombrero forward, in a rakish gesture.

"My son the charmer," she boasted and the assistant nodded eagerly in silent agreement.

The cashier added up the total cost of clothing and the items were all folded away neatly in two large carrier bags. Margaret thanked them, as the owner walked her to the door.

"He's going to Mexico to do some research on his own book," she said proudly, reaching up to stroke the side of Randal's face.

"Oh? Is he an author?"

"A very good one! Watch out for his name. It's Randal Forbes," she bragged.

"Well then, Randal, do have a good time, young man, and maybe we'll see you on the television one day," he said shaking Randal's hand.

"Thanks, I will and so will you… see me on the telly one day. For sure."

The shopkeeper looked directly into Randal's eyes and felt a creeping tingle of indefinable fear slither down his backbone. Randal's cool fingers slid through his own and he pulled away from the contact. Randal frowned. For some reason there were those who could instantly tune into his dark wavelength. It had happened before and it would happen again. In this case it was irrelevant because he had no intentions of making a return visit. However, it highlighted the fact that there were always potential enemies lurking in the shadows. It was wearisome and he was tired of eliminating lesser mortals, using valuable spiritual energy, that could be put to far better use.

★★★

Randal spoke to Alison on the phone, just before he flew out to Mexico. They had spent a few passionate days together in London, the previous month, making the most of their short time together. He would have stayed longer but she was in the middle of a tour and had to go to Scotland for her next appearance. After that, she was flying to Europe, playing in some of the most prestigious concert halls. Her life was hectic and her public extremely demanding, but she thrived on it all. Music was her obsession and dominated her life but Randal was in her blood and she could not exist without him.

Each parting was harder than the last but Alison knew that one day they would be together permanently. She had stopped torturing herself about their mind games and accepted the fact that they were tuned in to each other's heads. It was a powerful infusion; a telepathic bond with an electrifying physical attraction, quite breathtaking in its ferocity. Alison had never experienced anything like it with anyone else.

She was excited about Randal's new project. She had been encouraging him to write a novel for a while now, even though he did not have a lot of free time in between studies.

"You don't have to do it all at once but at least put some ideas down on paper," she said, as they finished a bottle of wine after dinner one night at her flat.

"Maybe," he replied, knocking back the last dregs of his drink and pulling her into his arms. "Maybe," he murmured again into her ear, flicking his hot tongue around the lobe in a circular fashion, which knocked all literary thoughts completely out of her mind.

The subject was not raised again until he had rung her to say he was off to Mexico, with Clive, in order to do some research for his new book. She was delighted with his decision but not so pleased about his travelling companion. Alison knew by now that Clive was deeply in love with Randal. Even though she had convinced herself that it was not reciprocated, she still felt uneasy at the thought of them together in such close proximity.

"Clive's mad about you! I know you care about him but you're just stringing him along. He's just waiting for the right moment when he thinks you might return his passion," she appealed to Randal.

Randal laughed; a little too harshly.

"Alison, don't you worry about Clive. He might have the hots for me but he's not short of male admirers. He tells me all the time. We really are just good friends. He knows I wouldn't touch a guy with a bargepole. So, relax," he lied magnificently.

You're one half of me but not party to my legacy. Only Clive knows about my powers and accepts them. Not always willingly but in the end resignedly. Clive shoulders that important responsibility and I would be lost without him, so red-hot passion, here and there, is quite honestly deserved. Besides I'm not exactly averse to the feel of his hands and mouth on me. He knows instinctively how to turn me on. He's got a diploma in decadency; a first-class honours degree in same-sex satisfaction.

And it was at that very moment that he decided emphatically that Alison must never, ever know about 'the gift.'

★★★

Clive was busy packing last-minute things and discovered that he did not possess one pair of decent sunglasses. He would have to buy them at the airport. He stuffed a couple more shirts into his already bulging suitcase. His parents were in Greece so he was in sole charge of his arrangements. He wished his mother was around because she was so much more methodical about these things.

He swore as he stubbed his little toe on a footstool that was in the way.

Hell! Now it's bleeding.

He winced with pain as he hopped over to the first-aid box in the cupboard. He was just putting on some antiseptic ointment when the telephone rang, so he hobbled back to answer it, cursing again under his breath.

"Hello!" he barked in an agitated tone, wanting to get the caller off the line.

"Hello you too! What's got up your nose?" replied Randal.

"Oh sorry. I didn't realise it was you. I've just knocked my toe and it hurts like hell under the nail," he moaned.

"Oh diddums, does the baby want me to kiss it better then?" taunted Randal.

Clive thought of other parts of his body that would benefit more from Randal's mouth but he kept it to himself.

"It's bloody painful, so don't mock the afflicted."

"And don't make your thoughts so transparent. Your body parts will definitely benefit more from my mouth while we're away," he said with uncanny accuracy.

Clive took a deep breath. He would always be in awe of Randal's telepathic powers.

"Do you have to steal my thoughts as well as my heart?" whispered Clive.

"You should be used to it by now. Anyway, I thought I'd just give you a bell to make sure everything's fine and to remind you that our flights at ten thirty, so I suggest we get to the airport a few hours before, to check in."

"I'll get a taxi and meet you there. I just need to buy a few things and that's me fixed up," added Clive.

"OK then, partner, have an early night and I'll see you *manana.*"

Clive put down the phone and contemplated for a few moments. He could not wait to begin his vacation. Mexico would be his idea of heaven as he had been recruited to be Randal's constant companion and assistant. He had been roped in to help him write his new book in the role of proofreader. Randal's imagination was wild and his ideas way ahead of his pen, so Clive would also copy-edit the rushed descriptions and plots into shape. Randal was capable but his inspiration took priority.

Clive felt honoured and hoped that it would be the first of many joint literary ventures in both a professional and intimate capacity.

9

Randal and Clive sat on their hotel balcony, drinking iced lagers and gazing below at the kaleidoscopic nerve centre of Mexico City. It was a very hot day so they had taken some time out from researching and writing to soak up the sunshine and atmosphere. It was their second week away and they had gathered together a phenomenal amount of information in such a short time.

Randal had decided that his book should be called *Fiesta* because the central character would have a clear connection with its religious ritual.

After they had rested, they hired a car, driving along avenues that had originally been causeways that linked the old Aztec Island capital with the mainland. The traffic was heavy and frenzied, a hotchpotch of the sleek and the decrepit.

"Randal, just clock the loaded politician in that Cadillac alongside the scruffy delivery boy on his bike. How the hell he's balancing that basket of goods on his greasy hair, without it sliding off, is miraculous. He should be in a circus act or something," remarked Clive.

"The boy or the politician?" replied Randal flippantly and Clive laughed.

"Hey, there's that kid on the street corner waving a paper at us again," observed Clive behind his sunglasses.

"He's just scratching a living. I'll stop the car and buy one," said Randal in one of his more generous moods.

The aroma of stone-ground meat, different herbs, perfume and flowers, all mingled with the smell of dust, tobacco, Mexican coffee and chilli and wafted over them as Randal gave the newsboy far more money than the paper was worth.

"*Gracias senor!*" he exclaimed as though Randal had robbed a bank for him.

"*De nada*," replied Randal with a wide smile.

He jumped back into the car and Clive shook his head at his lover's spontaneous generosity. He really was an enigma; one minute philanthropic and the next psychotic in his revenge.

"I want to visit the National University. It's the oldest educational institution on the North American continent," explained Randal with enthusiasm.

When they reached the building, he could not wait to enter it.

"Clive, just look at these amazing mosaic murals; all created by Mexico's master artists," he marvelled.

Aztec culture and mythology were top of Randal's agenda. The history of continual human sacrifices and their need for sacrificial victims greatly appealed to his dark side. He looked across at the lava-bed known as the *Pedegral*. Beneath it were the ruins of some ancient culture and below that the remains of another, cloaked in eternal mystery.

Much of Mexico City itself was built of Aztec rubble and that fact alone excited him greatly. Ideas for his novel bombarded his imagination, and twice, in the middle of the night, he had leaped out of bed, from the sheer compulsion to write his creations down. Pages and pages of inspiration spilled over into graphic details. Outlandish situations and plots came alive, as his pen took on a life of its own.

His work was a mix of pure fact and fiction, egged on by psychic tribal memories of fatalism and suspicion. His head felt like an aerial, receiving coded messages from ancient civilisations whose voices were all clamouring to be connected to 'the gift'. He felt almost obliged to capture in words, the power and the beauty; the pulse and the harmony; the complexity and the contrast of this splendid, sprawling, overcrowded land.

Clive had a nightmare in the early hours of the morning, after a particularly busy period. It was extremely vivid and when he awoke, he pinched himself hard to make sure he was truly back in the real world. He left Randal asleep in bed and padded barefoot over to the kettle to make a strong black coffee. He lit a cigarette and dragged hard on its filter tip, blowing out the smoke in an agitated fashion, mulling over the different harrowing images, as he waited for the water to boil.

In his dream there was a huge firework display which lit up the night sky. He was in some remote valley in the highlands of Mexico, a very long time ago. The mist swirled around the mountain tops and slopes, as a large number of people made their way along the different paths, heading towards him. The pageantry was stunning and Clive's ears vibrated to the music as they danced ceremoniously around him, carrying tribal flags festooned with coloured paper, striking feathers and pagan symbols.

Am I dreaming or is this really happening? Who are these people?

As he cogitated, the huge crowd split into two sections and made a deliberate pathway down the middle.

In the distance there was a grotesque figure, bounding along the thoroughfare, with a trident and standard. It had two horns on its head and Clive held his breath as a priest made the sign of the cross. A striking-looking man stepped forward and raised his hat in the air, throwing back his head and howling like a coyote. His cry was answered from another sector of the throng, and then from yet another, as they succumbed to the satanic influence.

The demon pranced nearer and began to attack the priests, passing sentence upon them, as they fell to the floor. It wore a hideous mask and its eyes flashed through the two holes, hypnotising its followers and destroying its opponents. Clive froze as it smelled him out and swivelled around in his direction. When it was nearly upon him it laughed harshly, ripping off its disguise to reveal the face beneath. Clive covered his eyes with his hands, to hide from the monstrous glare. Its identity caused him to wake up with a start. He was breathless with fear and turned to check on the sleeping figure at his side.

It was Randal. The carnival devil was Randal.

And Clive whispered a silent prayer that he would always be on the receiving end of his love and not his wrath.

Randal was put into the picture over breakfast, as Clive related the gist of his intense, unnerving dream. He was not entirely sure how he would react to such a dark comparison.

"Well, don't that beat all? Now I'm the carnival devil as well as the main recipient of 'the gift'. Actually, Clive, it's not a bad similarity. In fact, I quite like it. Yes, I like it a lot," he laughed and Clive felt relieved but then miffed.

"Oh, you do, do you? Well let me tell you it didn't do much for me! Should we just stick with 'the gift' huh? I don't need another fiendish menace in my turbulent life, dream or no dream."

"Are you saying I'm a menace?" replied Randal with dry amusement, deliberately ignoring Clive's other reference to his dark side.

"You know exactly what I mean, so don't play with me. I'm still reeling from those flashing eyes. It was quite daunting. You were daunting."

"What are you worried about, Clive? You woke up before I totally hexed you, didn't you?" jibed Randal, waving his hands and waggling his fingers mockingly, as though weaving a spell.

"What if hadn't woken up?" asked Clive in a half-serious but partly amused manner.

"Aha! What then indeed?" mocked Randal, dive-bombing on Clive and knocking him backward off his chair onto the floor, as he fell on top of him.

"Stop it! Stop it, you clown!" objected Clive but loving the feel of Randal's body against his own, even in jest.

Their humour turned into a passionate embrace and the dream was forgotten as Randal reassured Clive that he would never be on the receiving end of his intimidating glare.

After a steamy session, Clive buckled down to working on the book. His thoughts kept intruding and impaired his full concentration.

It's always going to be this way with him. Whenever his psychic ability is questioned or challenged, even in a light-hearted manner, there are never any clear-cut replies. I'm left wondering in the shadows, speculating on the outcome. Deep down I know that he'd never harm me. Not now. I've worked hard to get his trust. I still wrestle with my conscience and agonise over his sense of right and wrong. God knows how many times I've analysed his scruples. But now I've arrived at this present level of loyalty, in acceptance of 'the gift'.

Randal showed him a drawing he had done of how he visualised the central character in *Fiesta*.

"His name's Francisco Rodriguez, supposedly a student of modern times, but really he's a reincarnation of an Aztec priest, who's haunted by visions and flashbacks of his ancient past," explained Randal.

Clive studied the portrait and thought it looked familiar.

It puzzled Clive for a while but when Randal began to talk about his next chapter, he became engrossed as they plugged in the ever-ready cassette player, to record his words before they were lost. They worked solidly for a few hours and then clocked off for the rest of the afternoon. Randal went for a shower and Clive returned to the charcoal sketch on the table. The man's dark eyes stared out of the page and into Clive's fixed gaze.

Just where have I seen that face before?

He could hear Randal messing around in the bathroom, making howling noises, pretending he was a wolf. It reminded Clive of his dream and the coyote sounds that the people made as the carnival devil claimed their souls. And then it struck him.

Randal's rough drawing of Francisco Rodriguez, was the striking-looking man in the crowd, who had thrown up his hat and howled in response. In Clive's nightmare!

Whoa! Now this is really spooky!

Clive's mind began to sift through the different segments of his dream, trying to remember if the character had appeared in any of the other surreal locations. He could not recall his presence in anything other than the one significant place of action, which stood out in his memory.

Did Randal plant him in my subconscious before I fell asleep, or has he plucked the hallucination out of my head, now that I'm wide awake?

Either way, there was no doubt that Randal's sketch of the vibrant Francisco Rodriguez was the same man Clive had encountered so vividly in his nightmarish vision. By the time Randal had showered and dressed, Clive was in a state of amplified curiosity.

"Just where did you get the idea for the image of your main character?" petitioned Clive in a direct manner.

"Pray why?"

"Stop it."

"Stop what, my little subordinate-in-crime?"

"I think you've been playing your mind games with me in my sleep," admonished Clive.

"Now why would I want to do that?" taunted Randal.

"Will you stop answering questions with more questions!"

"We are in a bad moody, aren't we? It's not my fault that you didn't sleep last night. Is it now?"

"Isn't it?" frowned Clive.

"Now who's answering questions with more questions?" teased Randal.

"Forget it, just forget it," grumbled Clive, totally frustrated with Randal's taunting and lack of co-operation as he made his way towards the door.

"Come back here," laughed Randal, as he yanked Clive's arm, hampering his departure.

He opened his mouth to object but Randal put a finger against his lips quashing any words of protest before they were spoken. He led Clive back to the table.

"Now just sit there like a good little protector, while I pour you a fresh cup of coffee and we'll discuss whatever's bothering you. Don't move!" he ordered.

"You'll only make fun again."

"No, I won't. Here's your drink. Now rest your mouth."

"See! That's exactly what I mean. I've something really freaky on my mind and it's always turned into a joke," sulked Clive.

"Am I laughing? Now let's get down to business," stipulated Randal, lighting up two cheroots and handing one over to Clive.

"What's with the baby cigars?" asked Clive, preferring a cigarette.

"I've decided they suit my image more. From now on, I'll cheroot my way through life. Now, what's on your ever-analytical mind?"

"Promise you won't mock it and tell me the truth?"

"I solemnly promise that you will get the truth, the whole truth and nothing but the truth, so help me thingy, or words to that effect."

Clive sighed but continued.

"It's about your sketch of Francisco Rodriguez. This one here on the table. Just take a closer look at it."

"What about it?"

"He surfaced in my nightmare last night."

"Really? Whereabouts?"

"He was the central character in the crowd of devil worshippers who howled like a wolf and then threw his hat up into the air, as a form of reverence," elucidated Clive.

"Hmm," murmured Randal, rubbing his chin reflectively. "I see. Now that's really interesting."

Clive waited patiently for an explanation but Randal said nothing and just gazed downward at the image. A perplexed air played across his face and Clive could not make his mind up if he was stalling for effect, or procrastinating with genuine puzzlement.

"You promised to stop playing silly games with me," complained Clive when no explanation was forthcoming.

For a moment Randal appeared not to hear him. Then he looked up and gazed directly into Clive's line of vision. The tender expression in his steel-grey eyes took Clive's breath away. It was almost suffocating in its depth and Clive swallowed hard, wondering what had brought on this sudden, unlikely display of emotion.

"What? What is it?" asked Clive hoarsely, trying hard to act normally.

"You've passed the test! You've passed the crucial test! This is so fantastic, Clive, and now everything's clearer than ever!"

"Test?"

"Don't you see? My creation came to you in your dream. I didn't put him there. You did that all by yourself. We're moving along the same invisible thread of invention which can only mean one thing. 'The gift' has formerly recognised and nominated you as my sole protector. This is *its* way of showing us both that you've been officially appointed. Welcome to my kingdom, Clive. It's now actually written that we'll be together; as we were; as we are and always," he enthused.

Each of Randal's words had a profound effect upon Clive. From the very first day they had met, as children, he had only ever wanted Randal and had fought his own many demons to arrive at their present stage of intimacy. Clive knew that whatever else he achieved in his own lifetime, would now take second place and be of very little consequence, compared to the honour and esteemed homage of being spiritually elected to permanently serve at Randal's side.

Randal knew his supporters and would keep them safe. Over the weeks he had spent in Mexico, he had despatched numerous postcards back to England, cramming in as much news as possible, in the small space provided. He would have written longer letters but he was too busy exploring and creating. The recipients were pleased to hear from him and thought it extremely attentive of him, to make contact at all, considering his workload.

He had communicated more with Fiona than anyone else because he knew that she needed his interaction the most. She would kiss each postcard, then hide them in between the lingerie in her dressing table drawer. She thought of him constantly and longingly.

I want to put my feelings down and reply to him but what if the letter falls into the wrong hands? I can't bear being away from him. I feel like I'm weaning myself off an addictive drug. The withdrawal symptoms of his absence are dreadful. I can only suffer in silence. I have to conceal my depression from Miles and the family and the outside world. Miles presumes it's solely due to Daddy's death and Marcus's psychiatric order. It is to a large degree. But I need Randal. I love him. Am I going mad? Please come home, my darling. Come back to me.

Randal had achieved the same level of duplicity with Lord and Lady Pennington as he had with his own parents. Fiona would be incapable of rational thought if she knew the shocking truth behind her father's death and her son's insanity. Randal had become her physical and spiritual panacea and represented a fundamental and efficacious remedy. The passion and tenderness he evoked in her, blasted all negative and dispirited emotions away from within her troubled soul.

When Fiona had visited Marcus in the sanatorium, she had taken with her several photographs of his time at Oxford. She hoped that the images would jog his memory but he just stared vacantly at the unknown faces. She kept on turning the pages in the album.

"Look, Marcus. This is you at Beaumont College. You were reading English literature and had such a wide circle of friends. See?"

Marcus appeared to focus but nothing resonated. Randal had done a first-class job of wiping all his recollections away for good.

Fiona came across a photograph of Randal and Clive in the grounds of Clarendon Hall. She traced her finger around Randal's face, lingering on his lips and their shapely outline. She moaned inwardly at the thought of his stiff, hot tongue, darting from one hard nipple to the other and his irresistible mouth sucking at her swollen teats.

Marcus frowned deeply at the picture as if he was trying to dredge up a past memory. There appeared to be a faint flicker of reaction.

"What is it? Do you remember? Do you remember them? It's Randal and Clive. Randal Forbes and Clive Hargreaves. Oh, do try, Marcus. They were such close friends of yours. You must remember them!" she urged.

She held her breath in the hope that it had rung a bell in his subconscious but the moment passed and he just sank back into his apathetic state. She sighed deeply, partly because she thought that he had been on the verge of recalling something but also because the sight of Randal had stirred a deep yearning inside her that could only be healed by his passionate lovemaking. She had stopped torturing herself with guilt and now she just lived from day to day, anticipating the next time that he would come through the door of the Hall, into her bed and in between her legs.

Oh God I miss him so much. I ache for him. Terribly.

On an impulsive moment of recklessness, Randal had put pen to paper and against his better judgement had written to Fiona from Mexico. The contents were outrageous and censorial but reflected his need for her sexual favours. He had told her to destroy the letter once she had read it but keep the meaning locked away inside her until he returned. It took every ounce of her willpower to burn it. She wanted to read it over and over again but knew it was far too dangerous to retain.

Once he had addressed and sealed the envelope, he then wrote another letter to Alison with much the same sentiments except he had toned down the obscenities. She would not understand that side of him. He still put Alison on some kind of abstract virginal pedestal, even though he had explored the most intimate parts of her body and claimed them as his own.

Alison would always be the love of his life, completely in tune with his physical and spiritual needs.

But Lady Pennington would supply the essential missing ingredient he craved to feed his insatiable appetite for a much older woman and the forbidden, decadent, female passion that she willingly displayed, each and every time they met; far away from the world and its prying eyes.

All the while Randal was in Mexico, he felt the pull of his rightful destination. He knew it was fast approaching and the anticipation excited him and imbued him with an even higher sense of eroticism. Clive was on the receiving end of it most of the time but it also poured out of him into his work, bringing sexual fantasies alive on paper. Randal brought his central character to life with a shocking mixture of magic and lust. Francisco Rodriguez was so darkly vibrant, that Clive could not make up his mind if he had leaped out of the page into the room or had vanished from the room back into the book.

"You know, Clive," said Randal one night in bed, as they lay side by side, "I've always been averse to devoutness."

"You don't say. I would never have guessed."

"Don't get smart. You're the only one I can talk to like this. Just listen."

"I'm listening. I'm always listening," murmured Clive, his heart tripping at the intense gaze in Randal's eyes as he looked into his own.

"My Mum and Dad, well, yeah, they're pretty conventional in many ways, but even with all that, they only attend church services occasionally. They never forced me or Patricia to go, so there wasn't any real pressure to conform. They had us both christened, mind you. I can still feel the splashing of that water on my baby scalp. It burned. I cried all through the whole ceremony. You should see the photos. My face is screwed up in anger.

"Burned?"

"Like some kind of weird peroxide."

Clive gulped before he spoke.

"Don't freak out. Do you believe in the devil? Or satanic possession? That's what… that's what Reverend Stainthorpe thought. He said you were possessed. Is that possible? Without you knowing?" ventured Clive bravely.

Randal laughed so loud that Clive's ear vibrated with the noise.

"I'm as much in league with the devil as Noddy is with Dorian Gray. 'The gift' is all mine and mine alone. You should know that, Clive. I'm amazed that you even asked me that question."

"I guess, but you have to admit, your benefaction is pretty powerful and dark," added Clive.

"Dark? I don't see it like that but I understand why you do. It's just my telepathic way of balancing the books."

Clive nodded.

"Anyway, to continue, when Patricia was baptised, she just gurgled and smiled and basked in the mood of the whole ceremony. Quite a different story," admitted Randal at the comparison.

"Patricia's the nicest girl I've ever met. Not because she's your sister. She's beautiful inside and out," confirmed Clive.

"Blondie's cool. She's got her head screwed on the right way. She knows about us by the way. I saw it telepathically," he admitted.

"What!"

"She caught us at it one Christmas in my bedroom but never said a word. We can trust her, Clive. She's no grass. Anyway, I'll tell her it was a one-off. She'll play ball."

"No, she's not a snitch. That's obvious!"

"My dad idolises her. She'll always be his little girl. She's much more in tune with the flock-mock than I'll ever be."

"Flock-mock?"

"The inept, boring, tasteless, inane, unimaginative, vacuous populace who roam this earth in ever-decreasing circles," hissed Randal with an ominous glint in his molten-grey eyes.

"We're not all like that you know," corrected Clive in a hurt voice.

"I know that, but the bulk of lesser mortals are."

"Am I a lesser mortal?"

"Sometimes. Like now. Asking stupid questions about my benefaction when you should know better. Especially in view of the fact that your dream collided with my drawing and I told you about being chosen to stand at my side. Why can't you just accept it? Don't question it," he complained.

"I try. I try all the time to please you," whispered Clive.

"Hmm. Anyway, enough said for now. I'm feeling turned on," warned Randal through narrow, glittering eyes, silencing Clive's impending reply with his wandering hands and hot lips.

A rigid dismissal of righteousness had always remained with Randal since he was a baby in the crib. He considered himself vastly superior to the many and he knew that he was privileged to have been chosen. More recently he felt that he was not the only one who had been designated. Instinctively he knew there could be others but, as yet, he had not encountered them. He would face that circumstance, if and when it occurred. First and foremost, he had his own destiny to fulfil in this particular transition. Amazing powers had been bestowed upon him and, in turn, he would be thrust upon the world to enlighten the masses.

I'm the new religion and I'll apply my legacy accordingly, reaching out to my followers collectively through my approaching fame. The voice in my boyhood dream said my parents had been used as host bodies. That's about right. It still doesn't stop me loving them. In flesh and blood terms they are my family. But in spiritual terms, they are lost to me.

After several more weeks of touring in a combination of public transport and hired cars, Randal and Clive began to understand why Mexico was so vast. They travelled through many small towns within several regions, forever noting the different historical, cultural and spiritual values within each territory. They had been to *Leon*, *Puebla* and *Guadalajara*, meeting a huge variety of people, most of them hospitable and sympathetic to their research.

Clive had become an expert on sensing Randal's sudden outbursts of spontaneous inspiration.

"Stop! Stop the car! I need to investigate this on foot," he instructed Clive, feeling the urgent necessity to inspect the area around him; sniffing out the air for oscillations or influences that escaped Clive completely.

Randal was never without a pen or paper, scribbling in a furious fashion, not wanting to omit anything that came through on his own psychic wavelength.

"It was in 1521 that the capital fell to Cortes, and Mexico became the property of Spain. They had twin objectives: mineral wealth and a conversion to Christianity," he lectured Clive, pulling a face at the thought because his literary inspiration was derived solely through the ghosts of the ancient cultures and was not motivated by any divine influence.

"So, it's pagan spirits of the past that provide you with the right data? What a surprise," teased Clive but his adoring face belied his sarcasm.

"Yup. I can't tell you how many times I've tuned in to their sacrificial rites and vibrations."

My mind just rejects all recorded holy conversions. I guess I'm creating my very own de-Christianisation of historical events.

Towards the end of their travels, Randal and Clive returned to Mexico City and stayed at the same hotel in which they began their vacation. One night, when they were having their evening meal, Randal recognised a lecturer called Miguel Garcia from the university, who had been very helpful when he had visited the campus, in search of information.

"See that guy at the bar? The one in the puke-coloured shirt? Anyway, regardless of his fashion bypass, he's a fellow egghead and is so interesting. You'll like him," assured Randal as he sprang to his feet and was practically halfway across the room before Clive could comment.

Within the space of a few minutes, Randal had returned with the tutor. He was ordinary-looking, in his fiftieth year and would be probably overlooked in a crowd but his intellect was quite remarkable.

"This is my closest friend, Clive. He's at Beaumont College, Oxford with me. Clive, meet Miguel," beamed Randal and they shook hands.

They were in the middle of a drink when they felt an earth tremor ripple beneath them and the floor shook, causing their chairs to vibrate with the movement.

"Don't worry, tremors are commonplace here," explained Miguel with a reassuring smile.

"How common?" asked Clive uneasily.

"Seismologists say that Mexico and Central America are part of the world's most active earthquake zone," chipped in Randal who was totally undisturbed by the activity around him.

"Wonderful," murmured Clive, as he watched the cutlery and dishes wobble on the tabletop.

"It's rather amazing," continued Miguel in perfect English. "This city would have disappeared off the face of the Earth, only it's cushioned."

"Cushioned?" repeated Clive becoming more alarmed by the minute.

"From the worst of it all by the subterranean sea of mud which it rests on. Even so, a series of tremors over the years have claimed lives and caused extensive property damage," elaborated Miguel.

"Oh great. This just gets better and better," muttered Clive taking a large glug of his wine as his hand shook, causing the glass to bang against his front teeth.

"You know there are three earlier epochs before the Aztecs, each of which ended in disaster. Nobody really knows for sure just how many ancient cultures are actually buried in the lava beds. Perhaps you've mentioned this fact in your book, Randal?" continued Miguel.

"Not really because the major link between my central character is strictly with his Aztec past. I haven't touched upon other things before that time but I have thought about it," replied Randal, lighting up a cheroot, his imagination stirred.

Clive listened distractedly, willing himself to ignore the rattling of utensils on the tabletop. He tried hard to concentrate on the discussion and was glad that they had moved away from the subject of earth tremors. He joined in as best he could.

"Randal feels angry about the Spaniards and their determination to conquer and Christianise everything and everyone around them and their total destruction of great works of art," explained Clive.

"This is true. Whatever is known of ancient Mexico has been ascertained from fragments, like temple ruins; items such as an odd piece of sculpture or jewellery from a hidden grave or something buried in the dust. There could be still at least ten thousand sites yet unexplored," replied Miguel.

"Fantastic; bloody fantastic," enthused Randal in awe.

"You take it all so much in your stride; earthquakes, tremors and lava beds," commented Clive admiringly.

"There's little else I can do," smiled Miguel, "apart from emigrating perhaps?" and they all laughed.

Clive would have been more interested in their conversation if the fear of a possible earthquake was not uppermost in his mind.

"What about the volcanic zone?" he braved, as he felt another slight tremor underneath his chair.

"Aha! Now that is our very own geological plague," replied Miguel.

"Plague?"

"You see we are sat above a great, mysterious, subterranean fountain-head of volcanic violence, which periodically rocks the earth. You know these tremors that you are feeling Clive? They're nothing new."

"They're new to me! How many volcanoes are there that you know of?" he asked, as he took a lighted cheroot off Randal, his hand shaking slightly and forgetting his preference for ordinary tobacco.

"Too many. Now let's have another drink and talk about this wonderful novel you're both working on. How's that coming along?" inquired Miguel, wanting to change the subject to lessen Clive's obvious alarm.

"Oh, it's Randal's baby, not mine. I'm just here for the ride. I help him with the copy-editing while that amazing imagination of his is on fire," explained Clive.

"Your 'ride' is just as important as my creative juices," winked Randal suggestively, touching Clive's hand and an electric shock shot through his arm at the contact.

The tremors had ceased and Clive's anxiety lifted but he would not be sorry to be returning home in a few days' time. Oxford seemed a million miles away from this land of many contrasts and he was looking forward to starting his final year with Randal at his side.

Eventually Miguel thanked them both for their company and then left. He had to pick up some papers from the university and was in a reflective mood as he drove along. Randal especially had left a lasting impression.

That English boy with the unusual grey sparking eyes will be a name to remember. There's something very ethereal about him. His thirst for knowledge is unquenchable.

Randal's appetite for information was voracious. He had never concealed his desire for learning but he had masked the real intent behind it. He would use his peers accordingly, both for their esteemed approval and to steer him in the right material direction.

His rightful destination was already written but he had to rise up the ranks in a conventional fashion. Through his written word, his success would grow and sprout like spiritual vegetation, resulting in the cultural germination and advancement of the human mentality.

Mexico would be the first of many countries he would visit in his eternal search for pastures old and new. When published, *Fiesta* would explode and 'the gift' and its recipient would do the same; reaching his relentless, ultimate, dynamic goal of stardom.

10

Clive sat alone in the chapel of Beaumont College and looked distractedly at the items of silverware, from around the date of its foundation. The architecture was eclectic; a veritable mix of Gothic, neoclassical and baroque styles. He took comfort from the familiar ambience and felt at home. He was somewhat relieved to be back on solid ground after the ever-present volcanic threat on Mexican soil. The only thing that marred his return was the heart-rending fact that he had to share Randal again with everybody else. He needed time to be alone with his thoughts and he knew that Randal would never enter the chapel, or even touch it with a barbaric bargepole. Clive sighed deeply as he cogitated.

Here we go again. Glad to be back but sad to be pushed out. Not that he's doing it purposefully. His popularity is staggering. He's got hangers-on coming out of his supersonic ears. I want to say to them that he's mine; that I know every inch of his beautiful body; every expression and mood; every dark deed and the recipients of his wrath. Trouble is, he's universal and it'll only get worse; that baneful benefaction he lays claim to called 'the gift'. Oh God, who'll be next? Who'll step out of line and die? And yet, I still protect and idolise him. So, who's the crazy one, huh?

Clive moaned and covered his eyes with his hands. He heard footsteps heading in his direction and turned around to see who was approaching. Giles Lofthouse, a rather unconventional but extremely likeable student friend, from Clive's particular group, came into view.

"Hey dude! Good to see you again! How you doing? You look a bit down. I'm not disturbing you, am I?"

"Just thinking," replied Clive with a strained smile.

"Do you mind if I sit here with you? I've been rowing and you know how tiring that can be."

"I don't, but Randal does. It's one of his specialities in case you've not noticed," answered Clive in a disheartened tone.

Giles could have sworn that Clive was on the verge of tears as he observed his watery eyes and the way he chewed on his bottom lip, as if to stem the possibility. *He's obviously upset. I'll try and cheer him up.* Giles pushed him in a playful manner before he spoke. "Talking about the aforementioned red-haired Adonis, how is he? Lucky you, spending weeks in his scintillating orbit! It's all around the college, you know."

"What is?"

"Randal's lucrative publishing deal for the new book. What else? The research in Mexico must have been mind-blowing. He's mind-blowing! I've always wanted to visit the places you both travelled to," enthused Giles.

"Well, maybe you should have gone with him, instead. He's obviously made a huge impression," sulked Clive; the oh-so-familiar, pointless jealousy was coursing through his veins, distorting his never-ending swirling thoughts and causing his pulse to race with agitation and angst.

"Hey man! I've got a girlfriend remember? Samantha? We're still an item," Giles reassured him.

"So why call Randal a red-haired Adonis?"

"Well because… well because he is."

"Admit it, Giles. You swing both ways. For the record he's well and truly spoken for, so back off!" he growled.

Giles was confused by Clive's hostile manner and felt the need to pacify him. "Whoa! What kind of reception is that for a good friend? I'm pleased to see you and learn about your Mexican adventure but you attack me without good reason. Is Randal the cause of you sitting here, looking like a wet weekend? Clive, your insecurity is distorting your judgement. OK, I do fancy him, so does everything with a pulse, but I'd never try and take him away from you. You should know that. It's not my style," justified Giles.

Clive felt instantly regretful for his outburst. *It's not his fault that I'm paranoid. I better make this right. I don't want him to suspect anything else.* Clive's expression softened before he spoke. "Sorry I snapped. It's not you, Giles. I'm tired and I've not quite caught up with life in Oxford. Mexico was a culture shock but so vibrant and, yes, working with Randal on his book was mind-blowing. He's a genius with the most unique imagination that's quite startling. It's no secret that I'm in love with him, so having to share him again after weeks on the road together is rather hard," he admitted.

"I understand. I really do. If he was mine, and don't take this the wrong way, I'd feel exactly the same. But everyone knows that you're his number-one priority at Beaumont. It's so obvious," comforted Giles.

"Is it?"

"Clive! You're *numero uno*. It's only you who doubts it!"

"I guess," he murmured, relieved that the subject of 'the gift' remained hidden and his possessiveness was the sole topic of conversation.

"Hey, why don't we go for a drink? Let's put that cheeky smile back on your face again. I really would like to hear about your vacation. What do you say?" suggested Giles with a wide grin.

Clive nodded his head, as he decided to take him up on the offer.

"Why not? Good idea, so what are we waiting for?" he responded half-heartedly.

After shaking hands and some platonic back-slapping, they made their way out of the chapel into the grounds. Clive gave a silent sigh of relief.

Phew that was close! I really must learn to control my emotions because my jealousy could loosen my tongue and reveal far more than it should. My emotions are secondary to the protection of his lethal legacy. Aren't they? God I'm unhinged. He's my world. I'd die for him and he'd kill for me. How tragic is that?

★★★

Randal was in a startling, creative mode, so he decided to rewrite the last chapter of his soon-to-be-published book, *Fiesta*. Like Clive, he was glad to be back on terra firma but half of his imagination was still bubbling under the earth's crust in the Aztec ruins. His head was also languishing in the Inca Empire, as he introduced yet another character to his already established ones. The imagery was so colourful that he changed his mind yet again and opted to create an extra instalment of adventure, adding yet more twists and turns to the overall theme. He was miles away in the middle of a key scene when Clive returned to their flat.

"Don't talk to me! I don't want to break this visionary spell," he instructed Clive, with his hand up in the air, waggling his pen for added effect.

"I've not even walked into the room and you're giving me orders. Pardon me for breathing the same air," complained Clive, with a saturnine expression on his troubled face.

"Then don't breathe."

"Maybe that's the answer," muttered Clive sardonically. *Maybe if I stopped breathing, I wouldn't be so tortured. It's only autumn*

1978. What does the future hold for us? He's just beginning; fame and fan mail by the sack-loads to come and groupies by the hundreds, hammering on his back door.

"I can hear your unnecessary thoughts so just be a good little protector and make us both a coffee while I try my best to finish this budding masterpiece of creativity," smiled Randal, getting his usual effective buzz out of Clive's jealousy.

"Make your own coffee! When I'm appreciated properly, I'll get back to being your number-one slave," he replied scathingly.

"Who rattled your cranky cage then?" retorted Randal, still smiling.

"You have! You and 'the gift'. Me and my role. Me and my insane jealousy. I've just spent the last two hours with Giles Lofthouse at the Head of the River. We polished off several glugs of vodka between us. His reason was pleasure; mine was torment," he scowled.

Randal stopped writing and looked up. "You smell like a bootlegger. I don't suppose you bought a miniature bottle for me, while you were putting the world to rights?"

Clive shook his head and waltzed off into the bedroom to change his top, which was stained at the front with splodges of ink from his fountain pen. He donned his favourite David Bowie '1978 World Tour' T-shirt, and caught Randal's shape in the doorway out of the corner of his eye. He looked amused with folded arms.

"What's so funny?" asked Clive as Randal's smile turned into a grin.

"You are."

"Oh, am I?"

"I just said so, didn't I?" smiled Randal disarmingly, the yellow glints in his eyes twinkling with amusement rather than sparking with ill humour.

Clive's heart began to thud with longing, regardless of his dismal state of mind.

"And you won't get around me with 'the Randal smile' either! It'll take a lot more than that to pacify me today! Do you realise that you've hardly said two words to me since we came back?" he admonished.

"You need help with the maths, Clive. We're having a conversation right now, aren't we? You've pulled me away from my main objective so what more do you want?"

You. I want you. All of the time. Clive moaned inwardly.

"You got me," replied Randal out loud, with uncanny accuracy.

Clive felt the usual heady sensation at being mentally invaded. He still found it all unnerving but eternally amazing. "Do you have to steal my thoughts again, as well as my damaged heart?" he murmured.

Randal tipped his head to one side as his smile grew even wider. "Come to Daddy, Clive and let me make it all go away. Hmm?"

"Stop buttering me up with quick fixes. I need your respect as well as your wandering hands and selfish urges!" he replied forcibly.

"Wandering hands and selfish urges? Clive, Clive, Clive. That's your perception not mine," responded Randal, moving closer with each word.

"I just… I just need… I just need to feel… valued," gulped Clive, stumbling over his words as Randal pulled him close until they were face to face.

"Now take a deep breath and watch my mouth," whispered Randal against his lips. "Are you listening?"

Clive nodded, speechless at the sight of Randal's stunning features so close to his own.

"You're my same-sex soulmate. There'll never be another guy in my life that will turn me on, or know my needs, like you do. Now I can't promise you one hundred per cent attention all of the time, but I can promise you one thousand per cent attention to detail in my bed. As for being valued, well, our friendship is priceless. Your self-doubt is dictating your insecurity; your pessimism is feeding your negativity and your worth is far more than your low self-esteem. Do you dig all that? Hmm? Do you?" urged Randal.

"Be gentle with me. I'm only human," mumbled Clive as Randal's mouth came down on his own and took his soul away.

Clive knew underneath all of his self-doubt that Randal had spoken the truth and that any uncertainty was born out of vulnerability but there had to be a line drawn underneath his never-ending instability, with regards to his true role in Randal's life. Alison would undoubtedly take pole position; she was the sleek and shapely racing car of his lover's Grand Prix dream, but as long as he figured highly in his hidden-life priorities, it would sustain him throughout their time on earth, because he was only half a person, and would only have half a life, without Randal's borderline love.

★★★

One week later, Randal awoke suddenly at three o'clock in the morning. He sat bolt upright and turned his head to see that Clive was sleeping soundly at his side, snoring softly in his own dreamworld, with a contented expression on his cheeky face. Randal felt the hairs at the back of his neck stand on edge. He rubbed his arms to combat the cold air that hovered over his half of the bed. It worked its chilly path down the length of his body, until his fingers and toes felt almost numb with frostbite. *What the hell's going on?* As he cogitated, a human figure began to materialise in the corner of the room, then started to take shape, rather like an artist's sketch that blossomed into a lifelike painting, as the brushes filled in the form, colours and shadows that imbued the artwork with life.

Randal's eyes sparked with spiritual anticipation as though they were receiving signals from a celestial aerial. A handsome young man stood before him dressed in full First World War uniform. He looked lost and somewhat confused. His thick woollen jacket was dyed khaki and had two breast pockets for personal items. An internal one was sewn under the right flap of the lower tunic, where a battle dressing was kept for immediate use in case of gunshot wounds. He wore a stiffened peak cap, with a leather strap secured with two small brass buttons. His ammunition boots had hobnail soles and an Enfield rifle was slung over his shoulder in readiness. His blue eyes alighted on Randal and he automatically aimed the firearm at him.

"Don't move or else I'll shoot! Now tell me, who are you and where am I?" cross-examined the soldier.

Randal remained motionless but calm. "I'm not your enemy. I'm a receiver and I want to help you."

"A receiver?"

"Yes. Only I can see you. You're out of your time and you need to return to your original juncture or move on. I can help you either way," offered Randal.

"How do I know it's not a trap? Tell me your name! What regiment are you with?"

"I'm Randal Forbes. I'm not a soldier; I'm a student."

"You look the same age as me. I'm nineteen years old so why haven't you enrolled? Are you one of those cowardy-custard conscientious objectors? What good is studying when your country needs you? It's 1917 and we're still at war!" he admonished.

"I'm twelve months older than you but we're sixty-one years apart. Now, put down that gun and let me help you," urged Randal, putting on his dressing gown.

The soldier frowned deeply at Randal's explanation and shook his head with disbelief. "You talk in riddles. How can I trust you?"

"You can because I've got 'the gift' and I'm the answer to your dilemma. You know my name so what's yours? I like to know who I'm conversing with. I repeat, put down your rifle; it's distracting and pointless. I won't hurt you so why should you harm me?" coaxed Randal moving towards him. The young man felt a compulsion to comply. *I feel I can trust this student called Randal Forbes. It's almost as if I know him and yet how can that be? He's a stranger but his face is familiar.*

Randal heard his reasoning and felt exactly the same way. They looked intently into each other's gaze. The soldier relaxed his stance and the rifle hung loosely at his side. He removed his cap to reveal a head of fair hair and cleared his throat before he spoke.

"My name is Harold Thornton and I'm from the Cheshire regiment. I need to contact my family to tell them I'm alive. They think I'm missing in action. I have a sweetheart called Emily. She's the most beautiful girl on this earth and I'm going to marry her the minute I get out of this hellhole," he expounded.

Randal took a sharp intake of breath as the identity of the phantom soldier hit home and he felt an electric current catapult through his body. *Harold Thornton! He's my grandfather! My mother's father who died just before I was born! His sweetheart, Emily, is my maternal grandmother who worships me; who never stops telling me how much she misses him, how much he would have adored me. He survived and married his 'most beautiful girl on earth'. My grandfather! And he's one year younger than me!*

"You look taken aback; somewhat shell-shocked. Are you sure you're a student, Randal Forbes, and not a soldier who's deserted his post? I wouldn't really blame you. It's hell out there; a labyrinth of filth; trenches with the stench of death polluting the air," grimaced Harold.

Randal pulled himself together and chose his words carefully. "I'm just tired. It's been a long day and you woke me up. I'm telling you the truth. I'm not in the army; I'm a student of English literature at Beaumont College, Oxford. The year is 1978 and 'the gift' has brought you here. Please don't be afraid because it's just a poignant window in time; a necessary anomaly in order to link up with each other," he smiled; the Randal smile.

"I don't understand. What is this gift that you keep mentioning?"

Randal looked at Harold with affection before he explained. Although it was Clive alone who was privy to his benefaction, he felt no qualms in revealing it to the youthful presence of his deceased grandfather. "You want to marry your Emily when the war is over. I can tell you that you most definitely will. You will go on to have three daughters: Margaret, June and Dorothy, better known as Dottie. Margaret is my mother. I have a sister, Patricia. We are your future grandchildren. There are three others called Heather, Dean and Shannon. You see, I never knew you because you sadly passed just before I was born," he explained with misty, grey eyes.

"My grandson? You're my grandson? Impossible!" insisted Harold.

"I assure you that it's not. I've been chosen as the main recipient of 'the gift'. I'm telepathic, psychic and clairvoyant. I repeat, the year is 1978 and 'the gift' has enabled me to witness this moment in time. Look at the date on that newspaper; the one on the chair nearest to you."

Harold did as Randal said and stood rigid, just staring at the periodical.

"Do you believe me now?" claimed Randal in a gentle tone. "Observe the photographs. Men and women didn't dress like this in 1917. See the advert for holidays by jet plane? Everything's moved on."

"Jet plane? But… but how can this be? I must be dreaming. Surely?" puzzled Harold.

"No, you're not asleep. You're just from another time frame. Don't you see how fated this moment is? I never knew you but now we have an amazing opportunity to bond with each other. Look at me closely. Why would I lie to you?"

Harold saw Randal's earnest expression and relented. He felt a spark of indefinable recognition. He was very drawn to him and knew instinctively that it was the truth, regardless of the surrealistic circumstances and the incongruous juxtaposition. "Well I never! My grandson! How do you do! Well I never did!" he marvelled, all previous suspicion and uncertainty cast aside. "Tell me, Randal, was my Emily happy with me? Did we have a good life together?"

"More than good; your marriage was a joy and she worshipped you. She still does and that love lives on in me; in all of your grandchildren."

"Tell me about your mother. Margaret, did you say? She would be my first-born. Has she a good life with your father? Who is he and does he treat her well?"

"They're as happy together as you were with Emily. We're a close family; all of us look out for each other. My father's Edward Forbes and he's head of English in a grammar school. My mother's a music teacher and also gives private piano lessons at home. They all still live in Cheshire, not far from your beautiful wife."

"But my Emily's alone. How does she manage? I hate to think of her on her own. Is she lonely?"

"That she will never be; not as long as I draw breath."

"Are you so close to her? It's unusual for a chap of your age to care that much for an older relative. You're a very handsome young man even though your hair is far too long. You have your own life but your words are of such comfort to me. Tell me, Randal, does she know about your gift? Will you tell her that you've spoken to me?"

"I can't. My benefaction's a secret and she wouldn't believe in such things. I'm sorry but as much as I'd love to share this experience with her, I can't reveal it but take comfort from our talk. We've linked up by courtesy of 'the gift'. It's brought you to me; in this room; at this time," enthused Randal.

They shook hands and then hugged each other tightly. "My grandson! Well I never did!" repeated Harold but his image was fading fast and then it vanished.

Clive stirred and turned over to hold Randal only to find his side of the bed empty. He sat up, rubbed his eyes and spotted him in the middle of the room, with his back towards him and his arms wrapped around thin air. Clive frowned. "What's the matter? What are you doing?" he asked.

"Nothing. I just had a vision," murmured Randal.

"You and your imagination. You need to sleep so back to bed, maestro. Please?"

"Give me a minute. I'm just thinking." *Bye, Gramps. Hurry home and marry your Emily. She's waiting for you. We all are. It was an honour to meet you. Now rest in peace.*

Clive repeated his request but Randal was still side-tracked and lost in the moment. He felt quite humbled to have encountered his grandfather's spirit, an alien emotion, considering he was always full to the brim of his own self-importance. He experienced a sudden need to visit his family more often. *Hmm. Am I an egoist or an altruist? It's possible to be both I guess; a bit paradoxical but viable. I'll make time to visit them all next weekend. I feel almost obliged to do just that; specially to see Gran. I wish I could tell her about Gramps but that's out the question I'm afraid. Shame really. But she'll be with him again, one day anyway. At some point.*

"Are you receiving me or do I have to drag you back to bed?" urged Clive.

"What? Oh yeah... bed... gotcha," replied Randal distractedly as he made his way over with a glazed expression, the yellow glints in his eyes still glistening with a spiritual afterglow.

"What's going on in that genius head of yours now? Anything I can share?" puzzled Clive.

"Share?"

"Yes. Share, as in care."

Randal took off his dressing gown and then tumbled into his side of the bed. He cuddled up to Clive so that they were face to face.

"Do you fancy coming with me to Didsbury at the weekend? I thought I'd have some family time. You could call on your Mum and Dad as well?"

Clive began to tremble at the earnest, tender expression in his idol's eyes but mostly at the feel of Randal's naked body pressed up against his own.

"What's brought this on? I thought we were going to Giles's birthday party on Saturday night. You've been looking forward to it."

"I've changed my priorities," murmured Randal against Clive's lips.

Clive found it hard to speak. His body went into worshipping-Randal mode and his heart was hammering through his chest wall.

"Well? Are you coming with me?" repeated Randal suggestively.

"Yes, and yes," croaked Clive.

"Yes, and yes?"

"Yes, to Didsbury and yes to now."

"Why, Mr Hargreaves, what do you mean? Elaborate please."

The repartee stopped right there as a passionate clinch followed and they both succumbed to their carnal needs. In Clive's case it was pure love and endless devotion. In Randal's case it was out-and-out lust and experimentation, although he did care a lot about Clive's welfare. Either way they were lost in space and time.

★★★

Patricia pouted in the mirror and then added another layer of pink lip gloss to her shapely mouth. She knew she looked good, as she swung her body round to inspect the way her jeans hugged her petite bottom and long legs. Her blonde hair whirled around her beautiful face and the fringe rested just above her powder-blue eyes. Her heart skipped a beat and then she scolded herself for being overly excited. *Anyone would think he was my boyfriend, not my brother, but I've missed him terribly and it's always a blast when he's home, even for one weekend. Mum's on a high and Dad's stockpiling the Bordeaux and Chianti like it's going out of fashion. I can't wait! Oh! I hear a car. Let's see. It's him!*

Patricia fled down the stairs and through the front door as Randal parked up and turned off the ignition. He got out of the car only to be accosted, as she literally flung herself into his welcoming embrace.

"Something tells me you're glad I'm home," he quipped as she kissed his cheek repeatedly.

"Oh, I am, I am, I am! It's been too long since we hung out. Oxford's a thief. It's robbed me of my brother's special smile," she grinned.

"Very poetical. I may just plagiarise that line. My little sister, all grown up and spouting original quotes," he praised.

She caught the scent of his exquisite aftershave, as he hugged her again. *He looks incredible. Why can't I find a guy like him? All my boyfriends are second-rate. I know he's my flesh and blood but he fascinates me and I could look at him all day long. He's like a stunning male model with a superior intellect.*

"You look good, blondie. Arm-candy with a brain," he smiled disarmingly.

"I was just thinking the same about you! Maybe it's telepathy, huh?" she joked, but she was unknowingly right on the button.

They walked up the path arm in arm, only to be wildly greeted at the doorstep by their overjoyed mother, who could not wait to see her precious first-born.

"Hi Mum, how's it going?"

"Oh Randal, it's so good to see you again! Welcome home and give your mum a much-needed hug," beamed Margaret.

"One much-needed hug coming up. If this is the kind of reception I get, then I'll come home more often. It's a good job it doesn't go to my head."

"Not much!" Patricia joshed. "It's a wonder your head fits through the door!"

"Are you saying I'm full of it, my little sister-in-alms?" he teased.

"Well if the cap fits!"

"But it wouldn't. My head's far too big. Remember?"

They all laughed out loud as they entered the porch, a trio of close-knit kinsfolk.

"Where's Dad?" queried Randal as they stepped into the hallway.

"He's with your Uncle Ashley. They're stocking up on wine because I've asked the family round tonight. I hope you don't mind but they really would love to see you and hear about your Mexican travels," she enthused.

"The family? Does that include the 'bitter one'? Cousin-Spencer-the-supercilious? The boorish barrister-in-waiting?"

"I'm not sure if he's coming, but if he does, please don't bicker. Your father and uncle loathe it when you argue. Don't spoil everything by sniping at your cousin. It's so upsetting and unnecessary. Try to be civil," sighed Margaret.

"I am civil. I always insult him politely."

Patricia giggled and Margaret gave her a scathing look. "Let's face it, Mum. Randal's got his measure. Spencer's a pain. He thinks he's way above us all and gets some kind of sadistic pleasure from trying to bring Randal down, but he can't win and that's what sends him over the edge," Patricia expounded.

"He can be a little snooty at times, I guess," admitted Margaret.

"You guess? He makes snobbery into an art form but he's so acerbic that even elitism takes a back seat to condescension," spouted Randal.

Patricia giggled again and Margaret's lips twitched in the corners. "All right, all right, I know you've got a point. Anyway, he might not come at all," she responded, crossing her fingers behind her back.

"I'm going to ring Clive and see if he can join us. I dropped him off at his house before. He's not seen his parents for quite some time," pointed out Randal.

"He's always welcome to visit. In fact, I'll phone Rosemary and Paul to come with him. We can have a good old get-together. I'm sure Clive will have lots to say about your recent adventures. After all, he helped you tremendously with your book, and witnessed first-hand all the special creative moments. Now, your room is still the same. I've not changed a thing apart from some new T-shirts I bought for you in the sale at Kendal's. They'll come in handy when the weather turns milder."

"Still looking after me, Mum? You just can't help it," smiled Randal with affection.

"Of course! You'll always be my precious baby boy. Just as Patricia is my treasured baby girl. A mother is a mother for life, even when her children fly the nest. Now, get yourself washed and changed after your long drive and I'll go and prepare dinner. I'm making your favourite. Hotpot with pickled cabbage," she fussed.

"Hotpot with pickled cabbage, eh? I've not had that since I was ten years old."

"I know. But you loved it. And I love you," she smiled widely, standing on tiptoes to kiss his cheek and then making her way to the kitchen.

Oh mother, your precious baby boy has 'the gift'. You haven't got a clue but it's just as well. Just think of me with maternal warmth as I set the fucking world on fire.

Later that evening the house rang out with conversation and laughter. Randal's paternal family were striking up a familiar rapport with his maternal side, reminiscent of the old days. Randal was sitting in the same cosy armchair that he befriended as a child. It was his thinking seat; the personification of collusive planning in comfort; the nucleus of his devastating removal scripts; the deadly mental starting point that demolished Alice Hardman and John Sterling with telepathic liquidation.

He lit up a cheroot and inhaled deeply, then blew out a stream of smoke as he remembered. *Talk about armchair theatre! My earliest inanimate friend still steeped in paranormal vibrations. You served me well while I created those homicidal scripts in comfort. The chair that gave birth to 'the gift'.*

"Randal, what was the name of the hotel you and Clive stayed in when you first arrived in Mexico?" asked Margaret, interrupting his death-dealing recollections.

"Huh?"

"The hotel, what was its name?" she repeated.

"What hotel?"

"The Maya," piped up Clive when he saw that Randal was miles away. "It was ideal; slap bang in the centre of the city with everything to hand. We had such a good time there, didn't we, Rand?"

Randal nodded as he came back down to earth. A switch flicked back on as he acclimatised to the present scene and subject. A vivid recollection flashed through his brain of him and Clive thrashing around in the hotel bed, in between creating the chapters of his book. Randal looked across at him with a penetrating gaze as he spoke. "We had an amazing time there. We were like one and I couldn't have reached the ultimate climax of the story without you," he fawned.

The twofold meaning played havoc with Clive's sense of eroticism and his heart double-leaped at the sexual intimation. The inference went right over Margaret's head and did not resonate with the rest of the family as such, but Patricia saw right through the implication. *Good grief they're still at it! Clive's besotted, totally obsessed, and Randal's pressing all of his same-sex buttons.* "How's Alison?" she purposefully asked out loud, feeling miffed by proxy.

Randal picked up on her awareness but played it cool. "She's in Rome, on tour. I saw her just before she left. We get together when we can. Unfortunately, it's not too often."

"Give her my love when you speak to her next time. I saw her on the telly recently and she's more beautiful than ever. Don't you think so, Clive?" pumped Patricia with intentional guile.

"What? Oh yeah… absolutely," he agreed, trying very hard to disguise his jealousy.

"Randal wants to marry her, don't you?" stated his young cousin Dean, with a cheeky grin across his handsome little face.

"One day," smiled Randal and Clive's chest tightened with resentment and envy.

"It's far too soon for a serious relationship, don't you think?" queried his Aunty Dottie. "Just look at you! You could have the cream of the crop. It's a wonder all the girls aren't queuing up outside your flat in Oxford on a daily basis," she laughed.

"They are," sighed Clive deeply, looking at Dottie with a helpless expression.

"Oh, Clive, I'm sorry. I'm sure you have many girls wanting to go out with you too," apologised Dottie, kicking herself for ignoring his feelings. *Oh Lord, now I've made him feel inadequate. He looks so upset.*

Clive's despondent appearance had nothing to do with the dating popularity stakes. He was steadily training himself to cope with the endless stream of students tripping over themselves to impress Randal; to ignore the open-mouthed, glassy-eyed air of the countless followers who worshipped at Randal's foxy feet. Clive's dispirited look was all to do with Alison Whitaker because he now knew, beyond any shadow of a doubt, that she was destined to be Mrs Randal Forbes.

"Your Aunty Dottie's right, Randal. Your father and I are extremely fond of Alison but your education comes first. You're far too young to be serious with one girl but if you decide that she's the one for you, after you've graduated, and found your true vocation, then so be it," lectured Margaret.

"What is this? An Agony Aunt convention? Come on, Mum, lighten up. Let's have a drink and a laugh and kick the sermon into touch."

"Quite right, son," intercepted Edward. "Have some more wine. You too, Clive," he added as he refilled their glasses.

Dean left his lemonade on the table and then sat on the arm of Randal's chair, and kissed his cheek in a gesture of affection.

"I wish you'd come home a lot more to see me," he sulked.

Randal smiled winningly and stroked Dean's hair back off his face. "You've got pickled cabbage on the front of your sweatshirt. You better wash it off or else it'll stain. Go and ask your mum to wipe it away. OK, little buddy?"

"Don't care. I'd rather be with you."

"Would you now?"

Randal tickled Dean's tummy and he wriggled and giggled so much that he slid off the edge of the chair right into Randal's lap.

"Stop it… stop it," cackled Dean but he was really enjoying clowning around, loving every second of Randal's attention.

Clive's jealousy went up another toxic notch and his torturous thoughts ran riot. *The green-eyed monster raises its ugly head again over his twelve-year-old cousin! Who else? His parents? His sister? His aunt? I'm even resentful of his Champs Elysees briefs because they're permanently against his perfect prick! Everything was under control until the Alison comment. He's going to marry her! That's what's done it! That's what's set it all off again. Damn her! Damn him! Damn it all!*

Randal could hear Clive's rancorous and unnecessary thoughts. They were so aggrieved that he could almost taste the bitterness on his tongue. He stopped entertaining Dean and excused himself. Clive was highly agitated and preoccupied in a warlike world of his own making, so much so that he did not even notice Randal approaching him.

"I want to talk to you in the morning room," he whispered into Clive's ear, causing him to jump with the unexpected contact.

They looked at each other intensely and Clive knew that his rancid reflections were wide open to telepathic scrutiny. Randal's eyes glittered with restrained friction. "Wipe that pained expression off your freckled face and follow me," he elaborated through tight lips.

"Where are you two off to? I should have thought you'd be sick of each other by now!" observed Edward. "The family want to talk to you about your Mexican experience and to ask how the book is coming along."

"Give us a minute, Dad. I'm just going to show Clive a few pages of the latest chapter. He needs to check them over."

"Well, don't be too long."

"We won't," assured Randal, as he pulled Clive through the door by his elbow.

They sat at the breakfast table and the air crackled with tension. Clive knew that he had failed another crucial test. The silence was deafening. Eventually, he spoke first, his voice wavering with emotion.

"Don't start. I know what you're going to say. I'm sorry for my thoughts but… but I can just about cope with Alison as your girlfriend. I can't cope with her as your wife," he gulped.

"I'd never have guessed."

"Don't be flippant. This is anything but frivolous. I try so hard every day to be your ideal protector. There's a major problem though. I'm hopelessly in love with you so it gets complicated. If I wasn't, then I'd run a mile from my role. I wouldn't want any part of your legacy," he moaned.

"Here's the thing, Clive. You've been chosen to protect me, so it's far too late to back out. The fact you're my lover is coincidental but I want it that way. In fact, I more than want it that way. You turn me on, so don't turn me off. As for friendship, nobody else comes close. We've been over this so many times but I'm going to tape it and play it back to you daily, on a never-ending loop."

"What about Alison?"

"What about Alison?"

"Will you still want me when you marry her? How the hell can we be together when she'll be on the other side of your bed? How hard is that going to be? You've been part of my life for so long now. I'll feel cut in half," he groaned.

Randal's eyes narrowed with impatient vexation. The yellow glints sparked and threatened to ignite but he controlled his burgeoning displeasure. Clive recoiled from their threatening glow. He knew he had touched a vetoed nerve; the delicate subject of Alison should have remained unspoken. Randal would have understood his ungovernable thoughts on the matter but Clive had committed an unpardonable sin by bringing it all out into the open. The air bristled with dual displeasure, both of them taking deep breaths before they continued the conversation.

"Don't look at me like that! I don't know what's worse, your disgust or your wrath! It's just as well that I know you plan to marry her. It'll give me more time to come to terms with it all," pressed Clive.

"Just what exactly have you got to come to terms with?" hissed Randal.

"You know what! Her! Alison! Your bride-to-be!"

"You make it sound like a death sentence!"

"It is! For me it is! The death of our... of our... of us," persisted Clive.

Randal's eyes glittered with a new intensity and Clive held his breath at the naked lust in his luminous gaze. Randal lowered his voice as he moved nearer.

"Let's get this sorted right now. You need to take a long look at your debit and credit account. Debit number one, there's no such thing. Credit number one, you'll always be at my side; my lifelong friend, lover and protector. Credit number two, I'll never need another male relationship like ours. Credit number three, you get to travel with me everywhere and work alongside me permanently with all future creative projects. Credit number four, I'll probably see more of you than my wife-to-be. Credit number five, and perhaps the most important one of all, is that even though you piss me off to a dangerous degree, I'll never remove you. Take heart from the fact that your jealousy turns me on; in fact, it's such an aphrodisiac that if we were back at the flat in Oxford right now, I'd throw you on the bed and screw you so hard that you'd wish you were straight!"

Clive went into meltdown. His eyelashes fluttered and his whole body trembled with a myriad of emotions. He could not reply and even if he could, he would not want to spoil the moment by continuing to voice his endless possessiveness. They continued to outstare each other like a freeze-frame in a kitchen-sink drama; a motionless image that conveyed so much more than words.

"Hey you two, we're all waiting for you to tell us about the book!" interrupted Edward, as he walked in on them unexpectedly.

"We're coming, Dad," replied Randal as the spell was broken.

They walked back into the room with a silent understanding of each other's needs. This was a pivotal moment in their relationship. Clive would now dismiss any doubts about his role. The time had come for the unconditional acceptance of

Randal's rules. Stardom was looming and Clive would be an integral, irreplaceable part of that celebrity on many levels, when Randal achieved his lifelong ambitious goal.

Fame.

Epilogue

Randal sat at the ramshackle table in his and Clive's rented room in Oxford and kicked off his shoes, which were just about fit for wear. He needed a shave but his imagination was in full flow, so any ablutions were abandoned to accommodate the excitement of his wild, inventive artistry. His pen embraced his well-worn notepad as he scribbled over the ring of a coffee cup that had stained the centre of the page. Nothing mattered except the concept of originality; the flair, the panache and the innovation of his inception.

No sooner he had started one poem, another one began to take shape, leaving them both unfinished. His rancour drove him on and kept him jumping from one to the other. Randal despised conformity and pretention. He could not wait to rule the literary world because his main aim was to launch his own gift and be in complete control, in order to assist those who were struggling against the conventional tide; a benefactor for those who rebelled against the compliance of standards, rules or laws. Randal would be very magnanimous and promote the gifted artists who had been ruthlessly slighted or ignored but he would be absolutely deadly towards their rejectors. His pen spoke volumes as his words attacked the notepaper.

Too many fingers on too many hands,
On too many people, pull too many strings.
Too much confusion confusing the glow,
Not much illusion of things within things.
Strange men who sponsor your moods in the dark
Delude you with glory that's fractured with time,
Pump you with stale-crusted promises vile
Then lead you down alleyways, slithered in slime.
Mirrored disciples of tunes in their season
Draw straws in the corner through blindfolded minds,
Scratch at the surface with nail-bitten nausea,
Hellbent on Millennium, dangerous times.

He lit up a cheroot and his gaze glittered, complementing the glowing ember of ash at the smouldering tip. He licked his shapely lips. He looked facially stunning. His thick coppery-red hair flopped over one eye and he pushed it out of the way with his shapely hand. His perfect features were totally animated. He resembled an inspired demigod, totally seductive and in charge. He looked darkly brooding, adding an even further attractiveness to his breathtaking allure. He was unique and he knew it. He smiled the famous Randal smile as he read his latest work.

The circle closes rank around a sea of white shirts with striped ties
Haversacks of regulation weigh heavy on designer shoulders
Polished shoes and perfumed socks
Empty heads with dishwasher-smiles and brain-waste briefcases
Man-sweat fibres with ugly labels of tailored perfection
Sat on concrete thrones, preferring pretentiousness with smallpox
To the bohemian with a grin
Let the circle become broken with hollow gaps and spaces
Let them slash their baggage contents with no mercy or regret
Sabotage the shackles of convention to meet themselves going forward

And let their lives begin
If they don't wish to die.

Randal knew he was on the threshold of greatness. He had been preparing himself for world domination from the day he was born. He was completely confident about his exam results at Beaumont. He knew instinctively that he would sail through them and come out the other side in prime position. He would stun all of his lecturers with his grades. He had a psychic flash of his graduation day. His family would all be there with ear-splitting smiles. He could see the whole scenario as clearly as a sunburst in an unclouded, deep-blue sky. They would be brimming over with pride.

And why not? After all I've held myself back in order to go through the 'normal' channels of progress. My attention-seeking has not been self-centred. It's to show how superior I am and how inferior they all are. It's just a fact. They haven't a clue about 'the gift'. And that's the way it should be. In fact, that's the way it should always be. My family are still important to me because they are my flesh and blood on this earthly plane. They need my protection even though they would never understand my defensive methods. But I will be there for them when required and they will always be a part of my life in this transition. They adore me; rightly so.

Randal stopped writing and opened the desk drawer. He pulled out a recent picture of Alison which he was meaning to get framed but had been too busy to do so. She was simply captivating as she looked back at him through her beautiful amber eyes. He became very aroused at the thought of their passionate lovemaking. It was torrid and unbearably exciting. His erection strained against his underwear and he was very tempted to ejaculate all over her photographic image. As enticing as it all was, he had the self-control to abstain. He was seeing her in a day or two, so he held himself in check. The real deal was far more thrilling. Anyway, Clive would help him out on that score. He would know exactly what to do to relieve him.

He had another psychic flash out of nowhere. It was in the future and he was married to Alison. He saw a little boy; a miniature version of himself but he felt no spiritual attachment to him. The voice in his own boyhood dream said that there was no promise that 'the gift' would live in his children but if it did, he would know when to expect his special child. Randal felt sad, but not for long, because another vision blazed into his subconscious. A baby girl. A beautiful, unrighteous, red-haired doppelgänger, who dripped with telepathic venom and idolised him to the point of obsession. Randal was breathless with anticipation over the realisation that his benefaction would be passed on and nurtured in the rightful way.

This is fantastic! I'm elated! I always knew that Alison would be the mother of my gifted child. I recognised our connection from the very second I saw her beautiful face. But I can't tell her that. I don't know if I ever can. I'll play it by ear and see what transpires. Right now, I just want to wallow in the joy of knowing my legacy will be inherited. My own flesh and blood taking on the mantle of 'the gift'. How good is that? Just how good is that? Should I tell Clive? After all, his services will be needed to protect the little one. Just as he's always protected me. Hmm. Maybe it's too soon. I'll just let it all unfold, bit by bit. He's freaking out over me wanting to marry Alison so I'll hold back the baby news. His head won't take it all in. But it will. One day.

Randal finished writing and decided to spruce himself up. He showered and shaved then found some new jeans and a blue cashmere jumper that his mother had bought him for his last birthday. Clive came back from his lecture at that very moment. The sight and smell of Randal inflamed him. They both felt aroused for different reasons and that arousal was fully put to bed. Clive was now sure that it would continue throughout their Oxford education, into Randal's famed-filled future. And beyond.

About the Author

Fran Raya currently lives in Manchester. Her career has been predominantly in music since the 1970s, both in the UK and abroad, originally as a singer-songwriter but now in later years purely as a songwriter who places original songs with other artists. Fran is a member of The Guild of International Songwriters and Composers (GISC) and has been featured in their quarterly magazines. She has performed throughout Europe as she used to be based in Denmark and was the support act for Eric Clapton on his Scandinavian tours in the 1980s. She has also published poetry in numerous anthologies and as a result was awarded her own book, Thoughts of the Poet.